DIAMONDS ARE FOREVER

Eric Flint and Ryk E. Spoor

Cover designed by Laura Givens

This book is a work of fiction. Names, characters, places, and incidents either are
products of the author's imagination or are used fictitiously. Any resemblance to actual
persons, living or dead, events, or locales is entirely coincidental.

Eric Flint and Ryk E. Spoor
Visit our websites at:
https://ericflint.net/
and
http://grandcentralarena.com/

Printed in the United States of America

Originally Published in the anthology "Mountain Magic". Baen October 2004

This Printing: April 2020
1632, Inc.

ebook ISBN-13 978-1-948818-81-0
Trade Paperback ISBN-13 978-1-948818-82-7

Acknowledgements

No good story is written in a vacuum, and some people deserve special mention for helping ensure Diamonds Are Forever came out well.

My wife Kathleen, without whom I would never have the time to write

Zack Mian and IEM, who not only employed me, but gave me the knowledge of sensors and data processing that are key in Diamonds (and other books)

And L. Frank Baum, who created the Nomes and inspired their namesakes.

Dedication

This novel is dedicated to the real Jodi, whose magnificent singing voice, presence, and charm inspired her exaggerated but heroic namesake..

CONTENTS

1. CALLING MAMMA

"**Y**ou're getting MARRIED?!"

I had to pull the receiver away from my ear. Father always said if Mamma was in full voice she could break window glass over in the next county. "Yes, Mamma. I asked Jodi yesterday and she accepted."

"Well, that's WONDERFUL!" Another ear-saving reaction. Her voice shifted to *No Nonsense* mode. "Now you've put this off long enough, Clinton Jefferson Slade. You're bringin' that girl home to meet your family this very week, you hear? I know you can take that time off if'n you try, in that big fancy job that you're so important at."

When Mamma uses your whole name, there isn't anything for it but you'd better do as you're told. "Yes, Mamma. It's just . . . Mamma, she's city."

"Well, now, I know that, boy. What other kind of girl would you be meetin' in New York? We're not completely uneducated out here, you know."

I lowered my voice. "Mamma, I'll come. I'll bring her, okay. But . . . is everything okay there?"

"Well, of COURSE it—" Mamma cut off short, then sighed. "Oh. Yes, Clinton, ain't been none of *that* in quite a while. Daddy Zeke said you might be tryin' to hide *that* from this girl and that was why we hadn't met her."

"From anyone, Mamma, not just Jodi. Family's never told anyone, and I didn't aim to change that." I was slightly embarrassed to hear the Kentucky accent getting stronger; it always did when I talked to family. Not that I was really *embarrassed* about my family, not really, but . . . sometimes they were so weird. "So everything is okay?"

"Just FINE, dear. Now, we'll be expecting you when?"

I did a quick calculation in my head. "Say, Monday evening? We'll be driving and I'll have to make some arrangements before we go."

"That will be just fine, Clint dear." I was back to Clint now, so that was good. I hadn't been at all sure how they'd take me marrying a city girl, even though they really thought I was more than half city myself now. "We'll do you proud, boy, because we really are all proud of you, first Slade to finish college this century and all, and you done so well."

I blushed, and I know darn well Mamma could tell, even over the phone. "Aw, Mamma, ain't any big deal, really. Anyone in the family coulda done it."

"Don't you go selling yourself short, Clint dear. Even Evangeline knows perfectly well you're the genius in our family, and she's no dummy herself. Take care, and the whole family will be looking for you!"

We exchanged kisses over the phone, silly though that sounds, and I hung up.

"So," Jodi said, coming over, "were those bellows of fury, or was she happy to hear about it?"

"You could hear her?"

"*Oy vey*, Clint," she said, smiling. "Thought she'd break your eardrums with a couple of those."

Jodi was something of an anachronism. Her grandparents were immigrants who still spoke more Yiddish than English and had maintained an intimidatingly firm emphasis on the link between the old and new traditions. Linguistic traditions, anyway, if not religious ones. Jodi's grandfather had been active in the needle trade unions, a follower of Max Shachtman's brand of socialism. He had no use for religions of any kind, but that hadn't stopped him from maintaining a number of Jewish habits and customs. Jodi's family was almost a time capsule of clichés from the '40s and '50s, and Jodi had inherited enough to sound like a near-parody of the New York "Jewish American Princess." So why did I find her Yiddish, of all things, endearing? Especially when spoken with that New York accent that reminded me of nails on a chalkboard?

Probably just the blindness of love, I had to admit. I'd known Jodi Goldman for four years, though, so hopefully the blindness (or, in this case, deafness) would last for many years yet. "She was ecstatic," I said, answering her question. "I guess I should have more faith in my family, but they are still, well . . ."

"About as rustic backwoods as you were when you first showed up?"

I laughed. "Worse, sweetheart. I'd gone through college before that, remember. First Slade—"

"—this century, yes, I know, my fave *nebbish*. You mentioned it a time or two, probably because your whole family mentions it every time you go home, yes?"

"And on the phone. Look, I sorta committed us to go visit. You don't argue with Mamma."

"Yeah, sounds like my mother. When are we supposed to get there, so they can get a good look at what a horse you're bringing home?"

Jodi's sensitive about her height—she's taller than me by two inches or so, and I'm almost six feet tall. This doesn't bother me, but when she's nervous she tends to fret about it. As well as her weight, which for her height is just fine. "Don't you worry about that, Jodi. When they get a look at you, Father'll be tellin' me how lucky I am, and I'll have to watch so Adam doesn't try to steal you. Next week."

"What? Are you totally *meshuggeh*? What about work?"

"Mamma knows I can take the time off. What about you?"

She made a sort of growling noise in her throat, and then hummed several bars of a Streisand tune—a sign she was both thinking and calming herself down. "Okay, yeah, I think I can do that. They won't be thrilled, but if we want to make your Mamma happy, I can live with it. Oy, I have packing to do! Do you have electricity where you live?"

I managed to keep from laughing. "Yes. We have our own generators, actually. Every month Father or Adam trucks in to town to buy the fuel. Had to have the phone line run in special; these days I suppose we'd have done something like get a satellite link, but not back when the family first decided to get one."

Jodi blinked. "Running out a phone line just for you? That's pretty pricey, Clint."

"I said we was backwoods," I drawled, emphasizing my Kentucky accent. "Didn't say we was *poor* backwoods. If the Slades ain't the richest family in Crittenden County, it's only 'cause we've spent a lot of it the last few decades."

"I never knew, Clint." Jodi looked at me with surprise. "How'd your family get rich?"

I realized my big mouth had me dangerously close to the secret. Time to follow the honorable Slade tradition of ducking the truth. "One of my ancestors, Winston Slade, made a ton of money mining, and brought it with him to the homestead when he settled down." That was, as one of my online friends would put it, "telling the truth like a Jedi"—it was true "from a certain point of view." If I'd done the casual voice right, though, she'd never suspect a thing. Once we were married, we'd be living near New York and just visit the family homestead once in a while, so the chances were she'd never have to know.

"Well, that'll be a relief for my more cynical relatives," Jodi said, throwing back her long black hair. "They were kinda worried about just what your background was, especially with your nickname."

I wasn't very surprised. "I suppose 'Crowbar' Slade does sound either like a real honest-to-god Good Ole Boy, or like a wannabe wrestler." Truth was, I'd gotten the nickname in college because my roommates noticed I had a crowbar in my baggage when I moved in, and that I had that particular bag with me most of the time.

"Look," Jodi said, "if we're leaving to get there Monday like I think I heard you say, I gotta get moving. We just got tomorrow to get ready. And like I didn't already have a busy schedule tomorrow? You know what sort of planning I have to do for the wedding, and now we have to schlep all the way to Kentucky." She leaned slightly down and we both shut up for a while for the good-bye kiss, which lasted for several kisses as usual before she finally got out the door.

DIAMONDS ARE FOREVER

I sighed and grinned. Hey, maybe this would be fun.

Eric Flint and Ryk E. Spoor

2. MEET THE SLADES

"**O**w! I see why you have this oversuspended monster now." A larger bump than normal jolted Jodi against the harness. "And boy am I glad we put the equipment in those transport cases."

"I wouldn't have pulled out of the driveway if you hadn't. You want to keep doing work on our vacation, I'm at least going to make sure you can't wreck half the lab's equipment getting there. 'Sides, that one weren't nothing. Right after winter you should see the potholes we get and have to fill in afore—I mean, *be*fore—we can really drive the road well." I kicked myself mentally. One night sleeping over in a southern West Virginia motel on the way and a few stops at regional gas stations and I was already falling back into dialect. Pretty soon Jodi wouldn't even understand me.

"No bigger than the one on Seventeenth last month," Jodi said dismissingly. I had to remember that New Yorkers are like Texans: their potholes are worse, their taxicab drivers more dangerous, and their people tougher than anyone else, damn what the facts might be.

"Construction areas don't count as potholes." I responded. "*Holy—!*"

I slammed on the brakes just in time to keep from going over into the ravine that now cut squarely across the packed and oiled rock-dirt roadway leading to the Slade homestead. Last time I'd been here there hadn't been a sign of such a thing; now it yawned, a raw gash in the earth, fully forty feet from the edge I sat on to the other side, eight feet deep on the right dropping to ten or twelve on the left as it passed out of sight into the old-growth forest.

We sat there for a few moments in silence, me waiting for my heart to stop pounding before I slowly backed the truck a few more feet from the edge, just in case. Jodi turned to me. "So you *had* to prove me wrong. Okay, that is bigger than the one on Seventeenth." She looked at the ravine with slightly wide eyes, the only sign she was going to let this disturb her New York sangfroid. "So, what, are we supposed to fill that in with our bare hands?"

"Stay here a minute." I reached down into the bag and grabbed the crowbar.

I walked to the edge, so I could look to the left and right. I could see, down below, the mound of jumbled dirt, trees, and rocks which marked the slide. The thing that bothered me—

really, *really* bothered me—was how straight and selective this was. The slide started about fifty feet up the slope, cut across the road in a perfect right angle, and ended about a hundred feet below. I poked at the dirt with the crowbar; it crumbled like normal, not too wet, packed hard where the road was. There wasn't any sign of the usual slumping you get when the earth's moving because it's gotten too soggy and all. The road looked like someone had just cut a piece out of it with a giant knife, like a Bunyan-sized slice of earth pie. I listened. Not a sound except some water dripping off the trees in the fog—and the fog wasn't common this time of year, either. Seemed like the air was colder here than ought be. No animal sounds, the critters were quiet.

Maybe Mamma had been premature. This sure 'nuff looked like *that* kind of trouble to me.

Well, no help for it now. I studied the lay of the land. Awfully steep in parts but . . . I could probably make it around the upper end. Old-growth forest has some advantages, like usually bigger distances between the trees. I got back into the truck. "Jodi, get out and wait a ways down. I'll try and drive around."

"If you aren't scared to drive it, I'm not scared to ride it. And it's chilly out there."

"I *am* scared to drive it, but I ain't leavin' the truck parked here neither!" I heard my voice head all the way back home. Shoot, this wasn't good. "Look, Jodi, sweetheart, this kind of driving's really tricky, and I'll do better if I'm not worrying about you as a passenger while I'm trying to hold her steady on the slope."

Jodi rolled her eyes, then kissed my cheek and got out. I knew she would if I put it that way; it made practical sense, sure, but more importantly, it told her I didn't doubt her courage, just my concentration.

There was one really sticky moment when the earth near the top of the gouge started to give, but I gave her the gas and bounced clear before I could get dragged sideways. With only a couple of minor scratches to the side panels, I made it to the far side of the road. "YEEAH! Try 'n' stop a Slade that way, willya? *Ha!*" I shook the crowbar at the silent woods. "Okay, honey, you can come on over. Walk around the way I drove."

"Walk? You need sidewalks here, Clint! This isn't walking, this is an obstacle course!" Despite her complaints, Jodi was making her way through the woods at a respectable clip. She'd done hiking before. "I—*yow!*" Her figure seemed to vanish into the earth.

"Jodi!" I shouted in horror. Damnation, I should have made *her* take the crowbar! I had the whole car to protect me!

"Calm down, Clint!" Relief flooded me as I saw her rise back into sight, brushing leaves and dirt off. "I was just being a *schlemiel* and looking at you instead of where I was putting my big feet. Honestly, you worry like my grandmother." She emerged from the forest and got back into the car. "Well, so much for my perfect grooming."

"Don't worry none about that." I dropped the crowbar back into the bag and put the car in gear. "It's their fault for not watching for the slide and preventing it." That wasn't true, of course, if it was really what I suspected, but either way the family wouldn't blame Jodi for not looking her best. And as far as I was concerned, she'd look as good in jeans and a dirty T-shirt as in a formal gown.

There were no more incidents on the way up. We crested the last hill, came around the much smoother bend that led to Slade's Hollow, and came down through the woods into the open. "Whoa!" said Jodi involuntarily.

I couldn't repress a grin. "Yeah, y'all expected a couple log cabins and an outhouse, didn't you? Admit it, the Slades don't have a half-bad spread."

The Slade House really is something of a mansion, even if it is more spread out than up. Every generation adds a room or two somewhere, sorta like Lord Valentine's Castle. We try to keep a sort of style to it, but you can still tell where one generation left off and another started. The main part used for living these days was a massive mansion whose architecture was natural-looking logs and hewn stone—sort of a magnified version of what the earlier stuff had been, but if you knew anything about building you could tell that this thing hadn't been raised up by two farmers and their families; serious construction work had gone into the three-story, semicircular building.

"The original house is that small squarish part, off-center," I told Jodi, pointing. "That's where Winston Slade put his house back in 1802. It's used mostly for storage now. The funny addition over there is our generator shed, and on the other side's storage for tools, stuff like that. Got farm equipment in the barn there, even though we don't use it all that much—don't have to do much farming, so it's mostly just for the family."

"It's a mishmash all right, but pretty, you know? And this valley!"

"Yeah, the Hollow's pretty. One reason old Winston chose it was because it was already clear for building; figured it was a sign and built his house smack in the middle of the Hollow, on this little rise. And here we are."

I killed the engine and got out, Jodi doing the same on the other side. Our feet barely touched the ground before the front doors burst open and the Slade clan came running out, Mamma in the lead as usual. She was wearing her best dress, which was a pretty lace-embroidered blue and white affair that she'd only had to let out a size or two since she got married to Father and which set off her complexion and dark brown hair. There still wasn't a trace of gray in that thick hair. Either she just aged well or used dye that no one caught her at, but no one would have the guts to ask her.

"CLINT! Clinton! Welcome home, boy!" She gave me the usual huge hug and a kiss on the cheek, and turned to Jodi. "And this must be your Jodi! Welcome t' the Hollow, dear. Come on in, come on in, you're just in time for dinner!"

Adam clapped me on the back. "Quite a looker!" he murmured in my ear. "What's she see in you, Clint?"

I stuck my tongue out at him and crossed my eyes the way we used to when we were kids. "Maybe someday I'll tell you my secret. After I've got her safely tied down with a ring!"

Adam chuckled at that. The girls have always loved Adam. Standing six foot four and built like Conan the Barbarian, with the best of Mamma's softer rounded features tempering the edges and planes of the typical Slade face, he practically had to beat the girls off with a stick. I glanced towards my fiancée, to find that Mamma had taken charge of Jodi—well, as much as anyone can take charge of Jodi—and had her inside already.

I noticed that the gate had now rolled across the entrance to the Hollow, and heard the faint change in sound from the generators. Someone—probably Father—had engaged the electric fence.

Father was in the big family room when Adam and I got in, trailing behind everyone else. He gave me one of his usual nods. "Clint."

"Father." I gave him a hug, which he returned, then clasped hands for a moment.

15

"Been a while."

"Sorry, Father. I try to keep in touch."

He nodded. Not angry. Just quiet, as usual. Father didn't talk much, thought a lot, and acted when he had to. He was actually a tad shorter than me, but built as solid as the rock of the mountain; Father didn't have an ounce of fat on him but still outweighed me by about thirty pounds. Still, almost no one paid him mind when they first met him, on account of his being so quiet.

A booming laugh momentarily silenced everyone else. Grandpa Marlon was Father's opposite—he filled a room with his voice and his figure, standing taller even than Adam, with snow-white hair hanging to his shoulders and a rough-hewn face that reminded almost everyone of Charlton Heston. Evangeline, all long dark hair and pale face, was in the corner curled up on the padded armchair as usual, reading and watching. I didn't see Nellie or Helen, but that didn't really surprise me. Helen was going to be married herself soon, so she was probably out, and Nellie was trying to match her stride for stride, so to speak. Jonah was staring a bit too much at Jodi, but I remembered being fourteen myself, and in her New York getup Jodi was a pretty stareable sight.

I looked at Father again. "Road was out, Father. Down near Snake Rock."

His lips tightened. "Not the weather for slides."

"My thought, too."

"Fence is up. Don't worry for now." He looked at the dining room and started to head in that direction.

Mamma noticed. "Zeke! Ezekiel Slade! No one at the table yet!" Father stopped immediately; you didn't trifle with Mamma's directions. "Evangeline, could you be a treasure and help me set the table?" She noticed Jonah. "And stop standing around like a lump, Jonah Winston Slade! You and Adam go out and get Clint's truck unpacked and get their things to their rooms."

Jonah shook himself, looked at me enviously, and then nodded. "Yes, Mamma."

Jodi followed them out. "Whoa, boys, there's special equipment in there!"

Mamma seemed to think about protesting that she shouldn't do any work, but thought better of it. This was the opening I'd been hoping for. I went with Mamma into the kitchen to help her with the food—as usual, there was enough to feed an army. "Mamma . . ." I said, letting a warning tone creep into my voice.

She blinked up at me. "Something wrong, Clint dear?"

"The road was out. And it wasn't no landslide, neither."

She busied herself with the roast.

"You told me there wasn't any of that going on."

"Well, dear . . ." she said, in the voice she used when she was trying to get around Father, " . . . there *wasn't* any of that when I told you *then*. Just seems to have started in the last couple of days."

"I know that voice, Mamma! Don't try no dancin' around this one! Just what—"

"Clinton! Don't take that tone of voice with me! I can still tan your hide, boy, and I won't need no help to do it, neither!"

I backed down; getting Mamma mad wouldn't help. "Sorry, Mamma. Did anything happen that might have . . . started it again?"

"Clint, we've got your wedding and Helen's, and ain't going to be no surprise if Nellie's and even Adam's come pretty quick. And of course we're going to do you proud, son."

For a minute I was completely befuddled. What the heck did all that have to do with . . . "Oh, for the love of—Mamma Bea, you *didn't*!"

"I just sent Adam down for a little extra."

I couldn't believe this. "Mamma, you can't possibly be telling me we were broke again?"

She was slicing the roast in perfectly even slices—something I never did learn how to do, even though I was in some ways a better cook than Mamma. "Broke? Clint, darling, of course not. But ain't nothing wrong with thinkin' ahead, is there? Takes a powerful lot of money to keep the Slades running, and what with building Helen her new house—"

DIAMONDS ARE FOREVER

I closed my eyes and rubbed my temples. I could see where this was going. The Slades had always been rich, but never learned to keep it. Spend it like water, that was the Slade way. Why learn about investment and things like that? Need more money, just go get some. I suppose I should have expected something on those lines—the last time the family refilled the vault was, as Mamma said, when Grandpa Marlon took his last trip, and besides all the living expenses there'd been additions and enhancements to the house, all the gadgets that the Slade clan loved—Mamma couldn't get enough of the home theater and DVDs (she had just about the complete *Dark Shadows* collection, an expense big enough to show up in the budget of any third-world country), and even Father seemed to enjoy his own time with a computer almost as much as he liked doing his woodworking—and of course putting the first Slade in a century or more through a real expensive college with no scholarship.

" . . . so you see, Clint dear, weren't much choice. And no point putting things off, so I sent Adam off."

"You knew I was worried about this happening! Couldn't you have waited a week or so, until after me and Jodi left?"

"Clint. Enough, now."

I hadn't heard Father enter. "Yes, Father."

Father took up one platter, I took up another and followed him out. "Your Mamma is who she is. Works hard to be a Slade even though she weren't born one. Sometimes that's not all to the good. 'Taint no point worryin'. Trouble usually doesn't come here, even bad times. Scared of the Hollow. Keep her busy here, shouldn't see anything. Right, son?"

I smiled reluctantly. Father always reminded me of Unc Nunkie from the Oz books; this was a long and involved conversation for him. "Right, Father."

Mamma's voice suddenly boomed from the intercom she'd had strung through the whole house. "Dinner! Come an' get it!"

Even though Jodi was an extra, Mamma had taken out one leaf from the table since Nellie and Helen weren't here, so it wasn't hard to join hands to say Grace. Jodi looked slightly uncomfortable, but the Slades knew a lot of people who weren't of the Faith, so it didn't cause a bad moment like it might with some families—no pressure on her to follow along with the prayer.

Then we all got to eat, which was what we'd all been waiting for. The roast, as should have been obvious, was only the centerpiece. Potatoes, green beans, salad (which didn't used to be a fixture, but me and the girls pushed for it), sweet potato pie, biscuits, well, just so much food we had to eat fast before the table broke. And then there were the desserts! When Mamma set out to show off her cookin' skills, she didn't stop until you surrendered. Luckily, one thing Jodi wasn't traditional about was food; I hadn't had to face the horror of tryin' to tell Mamma that she'd have to change the way she cooked.

Jodi had done the wise thing, and eaten small servings of everything. I just plowed ahead and ate from one end of the table to the other, and paid the price with pain in my stomach later. Then again, I always eat more when I'm nervous, and damn-all but I was nervous tonight. Bad enough I was watching them decide what to think about my fiancée, but I had to worry about what Adam had stirred up at Mamma's orders.

I started to relax as the dinner wound down. Jodi got up and insisted on helping Mamma clean up. Even though cleanup's a lot easier with an industrial-sized dishwasher, there's still work to be done after a king-sized feeding like that one, and Jodi was scoring big points with Mamma by showing that, city girl or not, she'd do her share. I just hoped she didn't end up washing the actual pots and pans. Willing Jodi might be, good at cleaning dishes she wasn't. I always ended up having to rewash the ones she thought she'd scrubbed. And if Mamma found a spot of food left on one of her big pans . . . well, it'd be the Big Lecture for me.

Apparently that passed without incident, because Jodi and Mamma came out with Mamma reeling off her recipe for the sweet potato pie and leading Jodi into the big family room, where the instruments were being dragged out from the huge closets on the sides or taken down from the dark-paneled walls. The family room was just about large enough to play tennis in, but what with all the little tables, big comfy chairs and couches and all, it seemed right cozy.

"I hear tell from Clint you're a damn fine singer," Grandpa Marlon said. "The Slades always been a musical family too; mind if we indulge?"

"No, please do," Jodi said.

"Join in if you feel like it, dear."

I sat down to watch and join in the singing. I liked listening, and I felt too rusty to just join in right away. Mamma was on the piano—Nellie was better than she was, but of course Nellie wasn't here—Grandpa had his banjo, Father a guitar, Adam the big standup bass, and of course Jonah had an electric guitar, as might've been expected. Without Helen, we were short our main vocals. The family did several numbers Jodi didn't know, though I could hear her start to hum along with the choruses, but when we started up "Amazing Grace," she sat up; I knew she liked that song. I'd wondered about that, like how she could perform in Handel's *Messiah* with her background—to which she'd replied: "*Oy*, don't be silly. First, I'm a terrible Jew—I eat *trayf* sometimes. Second, beautiful music is beautiful music. I even like Wagner, which my grandfather would be like to explode over if I said it to his face. But Wagner was a great musician, just a complete *schmendrick* as a person."

I've always liked "Amazing Grace" myself; but once Jodi started singing it, you could see that even the rest of the Slades hadn't heard anything like it before. That voice, that could fill a concert hall without a single bit of electronic assistance, took the old spiritual and made it Jodi's own song of joy and thankfulness. There was a hush in the family room when the song ended, everyone else having stopped playing to hear her last notes. Grandpa spoke, finally. "Young lady, if'n I were wearin' a hat, I'd take it off to you. As it is, I have to say Clint didn't do you justice. Sing just like the angels, you do."

This time it was Jodi who blushed crimson. "More like a bellowing angel. I'm a belter, not a real singer."

"Don't sell yourself short," I said. "You're the best singer I know, Jodi."

"Can she do the glass trick?" Mamma wanted to know.

"Mamma!"

Jodi laughed. "Don't worry, Clint. Believe it or not, singers like me do sometimes get that question. I could, Mamma Slade, but it usually only works with pretty good glasses, and I wouldn't want to break anything valuable."

"Nonsense! I can always get more glasses—why, with all these young 'uns I've had through the years, I've gone through more'n one set of them anyways. But I've always thought that was just some fancy trick on stage."

"Well, it takes just the right pitch, and if your voice is off, it won't work. But if you really want . . ."

Mamma went to the cabinet and got out one of the leftover glasses from the set she'd had when I was young; yeah, I remembered breaking one of those. Only two left. "That one good enough?" she asked.

Jodi tapped the rim of the glass while everyone was silent. "B-sharp," I said automatically. She nodded. "In my higher range. But I think I'm loosened up enough . . ."

She put the glass down on the table, took a deep breath, and then opened her mouth wide, letting a single note build upward from a gentle hum to an almost deafening single-toned sound that escaped being a shriek only by sheer purity. As it built, you could hear an answering undertone, as the glass's resonant frequency was found, building, rebuilding upon itself, a positive feedback loop that caused the crystal to vibrate, blur, and with an abruptness that startled all of us even though we knew what was happening, it virtually exploded in a shimmer of transparent shrapnel.

"HooooEEE!" Grandpa and Mamma said at the same time.

"Wow!" Jonah exclaimed.

Jodi giggled. I grinned. "Luckily you use your powers for good and not evil."

"What about you, Clint?" Father said, as Mamma and Evangeline set about cleaning up the shattered glass; they wouldn't let Jodi help, of course, since Mamma had asked her to do the trick in the first place. "Haven't made a note yet."

"Aww, I'm too rusty, Father."

"Fiddlesticks, Clinton!" Mamma retorted, going to the trash bin. "Jonah, you get Clinton his fiddle."

Jodi looked at me. "That's right, you mentioned you used to play violin some."

"Some?" Adam laughed. "You know that song about the Devil? If'n the Devil came to Kentucky, it'd be Clint he'd be after."

"And he'd whip me good, too," I said, taking the fiddle from Jonah since Mamma weren't taking no for an answer. "But what the heck."

The lights flickered. A moment later I heard the backup generator come online. The family relaxed, but I could see Jodi was surprised by the change; for a moment, she'd seen the family in a completely different way. Every single Slade had stood, poised for action, and both Grandpa Marlon and Father had long iron bars in their hands—taken from concealed locations under their chairs. "Dang it all, Adam!" Grandpa said. "Who's forgotten to make sure the main generator's supplied again?"

It had broken the mood, for the time at least. I went to help Adam put more fuel into the generators. "Grandpa forgot that we drew almost twice normal load all day," Adam grumbled. "Mamma's been working everyone overtime. Shouldn't have had to refill until tomorrow."

" 'Don't think ahead, can't keep ahead,' " I quoted at him, checking the oil levels; I noticed that one of the generators was a new model, put in since last year; Father wasn't taking any chances.

"Yeah, yeah, I know. No excuses, just results." He tightened the cap down. "Okay, now we're done."

We went back inside, where Mamma had gotten Jodi to take her on in chess. I hoped she wasn't suckered into a bet; the only person who ever beat Mamma was Grandpa Marlon, and I more than half suspected that she let him win sometimes because his pride couldn't take the constant humiliation of having his daughter-in-law take him to the cleaners every time they played. I'm not that bad, but Mamma could beat me while she was busy watching TV. I studied the board, realizing that I'd actually never played Jodi. They were already past the point where I tended to concede to Mamma; looked like either Jodi was a heck of a lot better than I'd guessed, or Mamma didn't want to embarrass her by beating her too soon. Seeing the way Mamma was pursing her lips, though, I had to grin. Nope, she wasn't taking it easy; Jodi was making her work for it.

"Mate in five moves," I joked; Mamma knew I couldn't see more than three moves ahead even if I worked at it.

"Six," Jodi said absently. Mamma blinked and stared at her, then bent over the board with renewed concern. I repressed a snort of laughter, as I could see the little twitch at the corner of

Jodi's mouth that she always got when she was having someone on.

As that game was probably going to last a while, I went and joined Evangeline and Jonah at the entertainment center for a bit, taking turns beating the heck out of each other in the latest *Virtual Fighter* game. Just as Evangeline kicked me out of the ring, I heard Mamma's clear voice: "Well, now, I know when I'm beaten," followed by the clicking sound of her king being tipped over.

"Well, if that don't beat all," Marlon muttered from his armchair.

Evangeline finally spoke. She generally was even quieter than Father. Turning to me, she said, "You keep her."

"Oh, believe me, I mean to."

Eric Flint and Ryk E. Spoor

3. NIGHT MOVEMENTS

"**U**sually I'm up for a nosh before bed, but your mamma stuffed me so much I think I'm like to roll down the hall." Jodi stared at the three-decker BLT I was eating. "Clint, you keep eating like that and you'll look like Elvis."

"Thank yuh. Thankyuhverramuch," I said, with the proper accent. "I've been eatin' like this all my life. I exercise a lot, you know. And I know we'll be doing a lot of luggin' equipment around tomorrow, right?"

"Right. This is actually a good place to test. The New Madrid zone runs right through part of this county."

Jodi's current project was based on acoustic engineering research funded partly by NYU and partly by some interested commercial firms with some government backing. My main skills lay outside of that—I was a dual major, geology and compsci—but they intersected perfectly with the intent of the project, which was actually what had brought us together. It'd long been noted that some animals can apparently sense approaching earthquakes, and some work had been done showing that the Earth emitted varying levels of sound at different wavelengths ranging from infrasound—acoustic waves below about 20 cycles—and up to a bat-level ultrasound in the hundreds of thousands of cycles. Our team had modeled a number of possible interactions of the layers of soil, stone, and so on involved in fault systems, and it seemed to indicate that you should be able to detect both the main movement of an earthquake, and some of the precursors to it, through sound waves (rather than the related shockwaves recorded on seismographs). If the precursors could be detected, we'd have a possible way of actually predicting earthquakes. So if Jodi's sensor packages seemed to be getting reasonable readings, she'd probably just leave a set of them operating here; it was, as she said, a good potential location, with the fault system responsible for the greatest quake in the history of the United States passing by this very area.

"I notice," she continued, "we've got separate rooms."

"You had better believe it."

She grinned. "Hey, I'm not really *kvetching*; you wouldn't be getting the same room as me if we were staying at my house either." She looked out into the darkness. "Your family seems really nice, Clint. Okay, they are kinda weird, with this strange combination of hick and twenty-first-century gadget freaks, but they're trying to make me feel welcome, and I can tell they love the hell out of you. So why didn't you bring me here earlier?"

I looked down. Part of it of course was *that* problem, but it wasn't the only thing. "I guess I should've had more faith in them. I wasn't sure how they'd react to you. I mean, let's be honest, you're a—"

"JAP. Jewish-American Princess. I know, you can't say it because I'd knock your block off, but I can say it, because it's true. But I'm not like some of the others, and you know it. We work good together as a team, and did before we started dating. You do the modeling work and I do the tinkering and we and the rest do the brainstorming. So what's to worry about?"

"Some of the family's still pretty . . . fundamentalist. I didn't know how they'd take a Jewish daughter-in-law."

"You're right, you should have had more faith in them," she said tartly. Then she shrugged. "But I guess I wasn't sure how I'd introduce you to my family at first, either, and if they'd been like seven hundred miles away maybe I wouldn't have taken you to meet them yet."

I suspected she would have anyway, but I wasn't going to argue about this—since it might then get back around to what *other* reasons I might have for not bringing her to meet the folks.

"Well, you may still be hungry, but me, I'm just tired."

I walked her to her room, which was just down from Mamma and Father's. They might be being friendly, but they weren't taking any chances on anything happening under their roof.

Afterward, I went outside to take a look around the homestead. The lights from the house and the ones dotted around the property nearby let me make my way. Let me tell you, if you're from the city, you have no clue as to what dark is. The only thing darker than an overcast Kentucky night is a cave, and having been in both many times since I was a kid, there isn't much difference. Without the faint light from the homestead, I could've gotten lost fifteen feet from the front door.

A darker shadow against the night showed me where Adam was standing.

"Hey, Adam."

"Clint. Congratulations again."

"Thanks. Look, I hear Mamma sent you down."

"Yeah. S'pose that was a mistake?"

I shrugged, but nodded. "I think she should've waited until after we'd left. Nothing that desperate."

"Well, you know Mamma; once she gets an idea in her head, three wild bulls couldn't drag it outta her."

"Hadn't the place moved?"

"Well, sure 'nuff, but you know almost as much as me about that. Only so many places it gets moved to. Won't no one need to go down for a time now, anyway."

"You got a lot?"

He chuckled. "Grandpa Marlon was a little jealous. Got more than he did, last trip."

That startled me. "You got the biggest haul in our whole history?"

"Sure 'nuff. Three double handfuls. Stuffed the bag I had."

"Jesus!" The word was shocked out of me involuntarily. "Sorry, Adam. But . . . Jeez. That's going to actually take serious time to convert."

He laughed. "Not hardly. Sure, in the older days it was kinda hard but now with the markets open an' all? And the Internet connections and international market? I'd placed 'em with potential buyers 'fore you ever got here. Only a few left for us to keep for jewelry 'n' such."

I blinked. Yeah, things had changed that much. "Two things for Grandpa to be jealous over, then."

"Yep." He stared out at the fence. So did I. Was that movement?

"Father said something about the road," Adam said after a minute.

"Have to get it fixed. Forty feet got taken out by a slide."

"*They* did that."

I did the shrug-and-nod again. "That's my guess."

"Darn. Sorry, Clint."

"Guess we'll have to just hope nothing happens we can't explain to her."

"Or that we can hide it fast."

We both knew how important it was. If anyone else knew, the Slade gravy train would probably come to a screeching halt.

"Well," I said finally. "Guess I should head to bed."

"Me too. Forty feet of road . . . good thing we've got the equipment and supplies already. Might even need some cement to make concrete with, reinforce it you know."

"Might could. Won't protect the rest of it, but the whole area might be in need of that kind of stability. I'll help."

"If your lady'll let you off, we won't turn down another pair of hands."

"Heck, she'll help herself. She's got her own calluses."

Adam followed me in. "Guess she might, at that. Sure didn't have trouble carryin' her bags herself."

I went to my room. Undressing with the light off as usual, I kept an eye out the window. The moon showed now through an occasional ragged break in the clouds. Suddenly I saw movement.

Yeah. They were there, looking at the house almost as though they could see me looking back, two of them. Looked like they might be armed. But still, they didn't try to pass the fence. Not yet, anyway. I saw other movement near them, but didn't look too closely. There are things that give me the creeps when I see them, so I try not to. I pulled the steel shutters over the window and locked them. Even with that and the door locked, it was a while before I fell asleep.

Eric Flint and Ryk E. Spoor

4. ECHOES OF THE PRESENT

"**A**re we getting a signal now?" Jodi asked, having adjusted the reception parameters again and checked the fifth probe's functioning.

"We get signal," I said in a monotone. "Main screen turn on."

"You run through that stupid routine once more, wise guy, and all your mouth is belong to duct tape."

"What you say???"

"I mean it!"

"Anybody want a peanut?"

"C'mon, Clint, stop the comedy, I want to see if this works!"

"So do I," I said seriously. "I was making the last adjustments. You do the honors."

It had been, for me, a tense couple of days, as she'd seemed almost on the edge of asking questions I couldn't have dodged well, and *they* had assuredly been active. Like asking about the steel shutters, which we'd explained with older history about local feuds and some later paranoia born of the Cold War and survivalist themes. Fortunately she'd been with Mamma, talking nonstop about dresses and color schemes, when Jonah had come running in to me and Father to give us the news about the hole in the storage shed and the concrete all going missing. I'd made a virtue of that necessity, heading into town with Jodi so we could be together while picking up the concrete—and while Father and Adam fixed the shed so it looked okay. After getting the road repaired the last two days—well, making new road, really—Jodi and I had finally gotten around to setting up SUITS, the Subterranean Ultra-Infrasonic Tracking System.

"Here goes," she said. "Igor, throw the switch!"

The screen flickered, then began to show a multicolored jumble of lines and dots all over the place. There was a big central blob, some dark and light areas, and so on. To a layman, it would look like a modern art piece, but we could tell there was some kind of structure there. "*Oooooooy vey*," Jodi moaned. "Look at that, the signal's such total *schmootz* I can't make out anything."

"Hey, don't worry. That's the raw signal. Looks like the gadget's working just fine. I just have to clean up the signal. I could do averaging, but if we're looking for individual signals that might really screw up things."

"We're sampling at two GS," she pointed out. "We could probably take five, ten and average them without losing too much, unless all the signal we want is on the really high limit."

I nodded. "Probably. And it's already sorting by band . . . maybe I can take each band separately and focus on individual strong-signal regions."

We started fiddling with the various algorithms I'd already coded into SUITS. Slowly a more clear-cut image began to appear on the screen, although it would have been no less arcane to a layman.

Jodi stared at it. "What sort of cockamamie signal is that?"

I had to admit it had me stumped too. There was a huge zone under the Hollow that was . . . different. Signals changed going through it. I tried some analysis on it. "Dense. Really, really, really dense, Jodi. Specific gravity over five, at least."

"Totally *meshuggeneh*, Clint. There's almost no natural rock even close to that density, except—" Suddenly she stood and stared around her. Then she bent back to the display. "Clint, look—gimme a better look at some of the signals coming in from here. Yeah. Now, what's that say to you?"

I was starting to get her drift. "I think I see. That's why the Hollow looks like it does."

"One big mass of nickel-iron. Your Hollow is a meteor crater."

"Darned if you ain't right." I caught myself before commenting on how much sense everything made now.

"And look here, around the area—these deader spots. Clint, I think you've got caves running through your property!"

Ice seemed to pierce my heart. I tried to act casual. "Where?"

"Look. You know there's karst all over around here, it isn't unlikely. Isn't this part over near the road? Maybe that's why it slid, some kind of small cave-in or sinkhole."

She wasn't far wrong, of course. "Yeah, that would make sense."

"Maybe there's even an entrance around somewhere!"

"I'd think we'd have found it in the past few centuries."

She looked crestfallen. "I guess you would, yeah. Darn, but I would've loved to see a new cave! Well, at least we're stopping by Mammoth Caves on the way back, right?"

"I promised, didn't I? Didn't I know you were a caver? Just didn't want to stop on the way up, we'd have spent a day and a half there, I know you."

She nodded, grinning sheepishly.

"Anyway, this isn't helping us check out the real signals. I'll have to clean 'em up from the interference here, start trying to sort out different patterns, all that, and then correlate them with tremors in the area."

"Right, right. It's running good now."

"Sure is."

We left SUITS to gather data for a while, and went to join Adam, who'd invited us to go fishing. While fishing wasn't Jodi's favorite thing, she was a good sport about it. Me, I was just glad to have a distraction while I recovered from yet another near miss.

That evening, I filled in Father, Helen, Grandpa, and Adam on our discovery.

"By thunder, that explains it! No wonder they almost never tread on the home ground!"

Father nodded. "Good thing."

Couldn't argue with that. I'd seen what the back of the storage shed looked like. If that was what they could manage in a desperate raid, half blind and stretched to the limit, I hated to think what would have happened if they hadn't been slowed up.

After everyone went to bed that evening, I had my own portable crunching away at the signals. There were some interesting patterns turning up. I was trying various signal envelopes, filters, and so on to see if I could make any sense of them. They were clearly signals, not random noise, but it's always hard to figure out what a given signal is if you don't have a prior reference point. And these were pretty faint; processing could pull them out of the noise floor, but they weren't big, clear signals that I could rely on correlating with something else. Something about their general patterns seemed vaguely familiar, but the familiarity just wouldn't gel. Oh, well, I'd figure it out eventually.

It was the middle of the next morning that Jodi came running out of the house to where Adam, Father, and I were doing maintenance on the generators. "Clint! Clint, come on! You have to see this!"

"What?"

"Come on! You'll love it! I was looking over the whole signal plot and I think—well, never mind, we'll see when we get there!"

I looked at Father and Adam. They'd looked interested when she first came over, but their eyes started to glaze over when she said "signal plot." Father gave a tolerant nod and let Jodi drag me off.

To my surprise, we went straight past the house and started up Cold Breeze Hill. "Hey, I thought you found something on the plot!"

"I did!"

I followed her, a sense of foreboding building as we went up. Her footsteps slowed as she found herself walking a well-defined path, worn by feet that had climbed those very stones hundreds—maybe thousands—of times since the dawn of the nineteenth century.

Her eyes narrowed and I swallowed. "I found a signal pattern that seemed to indicate that a cave came very near the surface here," she said quietly as she continued to walk.

I was silent. We rounded the last corner, passing between Winston's Gap—two huge boulders that forced you to walk single-file.

And there it was, a yawning hole in the ground with the massive iron grate secured across it with a heavy steel bar and chained with a hardened steel padlock. The big metal sign across it blazoned Slade Family Property. Keep Out.

Jodi stared at the barrier, large enough to make a decent bank vault, and finally turned to me. "Okay, Clint. What in hell is going on here?"

I closed my eyes. Was there any way . . . ?

Not a chance, I answered myself. Too many mysteries, and this one just couldn't be explained away. Not with her caving enthusiasm and my evasion of the subject only yesterday.

"I think you'd better come back to the house. We've got a lot of talking to do."

Jodi followed me. It was not a companionable silence.

Eric Flint and Ryk E. Spoor

5. WEALTH OF HISTORY

Father started out. "All begins with Winston Slade."

Winston Slade had been quite a character. Son of a butler for one of the English nobility (family legend differed on just who), he'd run away and ended up in Holland, where he made a sort of living performing odd jobs until one of the local jewelers gave him a chance to apprentice. Winston didn't mind the work, but after a while his restlessness got the better of him, and he took his accumulated savings—what little there was—and got a boat to America. He arrived in 1795 and immediately started working his way across the country, doing whatever jobs came to hand. He had a reputation as a man who'd try anything once, and never complain no matter how hard, dirty, or dangerous. He fought Indians in the mountains, caught at least one outlaw himself, was suspected of smuggling activities, and joined a traveling group of performers (who might, some said, be a fancy group of thieves) for a few months. Finally he reached the interior of Kentucky and decided that now, at the age of thirty-three, he was getting tired of the constant movement. He found a girl who could put up with him—Genevive Vandemeer—and the two of them packed up everything they owned and set out to find a homestead. When Winston found the Hollow, he knew he had arrived. He built the house with his own hands and started working on becoming a settled farmer.

"Winston weren't exactly a wanderer," Grandpa said. "He wandered because he wanted excitement. When he settled down, he meant to do it. But it wasn't easy on him."

This made the cave he found some years after they settled a godsend. It gave him a dangerous and challenging place to explore that nonetheless kept him near home. Genevive didn't like it, of course, but it was better than Winston either forcing her to move every few years, or just running off into the sunset.

By the end of 1811, Winston Slade had explored a considerable stretch of cave, methodically working his way inward, taking different sources of light and taking far fewer chances than might be expected. He enjoyed doing his explorations especially during the winter, as the underground passages were actually warmer than the air above. On December 2, 1811, Winston descended into the darkness for a two-day exploration jaunt. By this time, Genevive had grown accustomed to his periodic explorations. She was no shrinking violet and as long as he left her a gun, plenty of firewood, and food for the time, she was perfectly content to take care of things for a few days. On at least one occasion Winston had come back to find a bear laid out for skinning, Genevive having shot it when it got too close to the family holdings.

Winston took a new path downward which, after a short steep run, led into a number of magnificent caverns whose extent he could hardly grasp. While exploring the side passages, he came across a cave dotted with fascinating pools filled with various types of stones. This puzzled Winston. He had seen "cave pearls" before, but this wasn't the same thing; each pool had a particular sort of stone in it, rounded as though from water flow. He wondered what sort of process would sort out minerals like that.

It didn't occur to him at that point that there was anything intelligent behind the pattern. While he'd occasionally heard odd sounds and movements in his explorations, he'd never seen anything to give evidence that there was really anything down there. He was the only man who'd ever descended this far into the earth that he knew of.

One particular pool, filled with translucent pebbles, attracted his attention. With the shimmering, pure cave water pouring down into the pool, the stones seemed almost like landborne clouds or ghosts of pebbles. Idly he reached in and picked up a few, rolling them around in his hand.

It was at that moment that he noticed something—a particular glint of light, a feel, he was never quite sure—that tugged on memories from twenty years before. Hardly able to believe it, he tried the pebbles on his jackknife; the knife scratched. The file he carried in his pocket, hardened in his own hand-forge, couldn't make a mark on them.

Winston let out a whoop which could have been heard for miles in the caves, had there been anyone to hear it, and scooped out the pebbles, stuffing them into his pockets. He considered checking the rest of the pools, but he was too eager to get out and show Genevive.

As he turned to go, Winston suddenly felt his blood run cold. He saw something moving at the edge of his light, where nothing should move at all. If he could have, he would have extinguished the torches, but he knew that if he ever lost the light, he'd never get it back. And did he want to be alone in the dark with the shape he could barely see?

So he tried to hide behind a large stalagmite. The shape came on, carefully stopping at each pool and waiting a moment before moving on. It paid no immediate attention to the torches or Winston, and it dawned on the ancestor of the Slade clan that the thing was blind in the normal sense. Clearly it could make its way around without help, but it wasn't using sight or smell. Winston began edging slowly away from it, and received confirmation that it could not, in fact, see him. Winston still moved very carefully, as he suspected the thing had other senses—possibly hearing, or something more outlandish.

The creature was making its way methodically along the array of pools, and Winston realized it wouldn't be long before it reached the pool he'd just emptied. It was then that it dawned on him that these pools must be something special to this creature. Maybe it was a miner, as well. What it might do when it found one of its pools emptied was something Winston didn't care to find out. The thing might be shorter than him, but its color and the way it moved gave him the impression of something with the solidity of stone. Winston grabbed up one of the torches, made sure the rest of his equipment was secure, and headed for the exit as quickly as he dared.

His foot struck a pebble just as he reached the tunnel, and the rattling, clicking sound echoed like thunder around the cavern. Instantly the creature's head turned in his direction, and it began walking purposefully towards him.

Seeing that stiff-limbed mockery of a man shambling towards him, Winston panicked. He spun and dashed off, hearing something like an unoiled gate screech behind him.

"Winston got out, of course, or we wouldn't be here to talk about it," I finished. "He and Genevive darn near moved out that day, momentarily wondering if he was atop a stairway to Hell, but the lure of money was stronger. Plus, with the relief born of escaping the things, Winston's curiosity returned."

"Whoa, whoa, whoa!" Jodi said. "What, is this the reverse of the old bit where the city slickers play tricks on the country rube? Are you serious?"

For answer, Adam pulled on one of the fireplace bricks, which opened a concealed vault. He reached in and tossed what he found to Jodi.

Jodi looked at the rough pebble. "Diamonds? Here? Isn't that crazy talk?"

I shook my head. "Turns out there's three places you find kimberlite pipes in Kentucky. One of them is in this county, not far from here. No one's ever found a diamond in Kentucky, but as near as I can figure it, the Nomes can dig into 'em at a level no one's ever reached before and there's diamonds down there."

Jodi looked at me. " 'Nomes'?"

I blushed while the rest of the family laughed. "Ayup, Nomes indeed!" Grandpa Marlon boomed. "Old Winston called 'em kobolds, or somethin' close to that, but when little Clint saw 'em first he was readin' them Oz books an' so he started callin' them Nomes, and their leader, assumin' they got one, Ruggedo."

"Okay, so it's silly. Still the way I think of them."

"So," Jodi said, "these 'Nomes' or 'kobolds' have been after you guys ever since for stealing their diamonds, like a leprechaun and his gold or something?"

"Something like that," I said. "Winston figured out a lot of stuff about them in the next few years. The reason they had a hard time tracking him was because he carried iron with him. Cold iron, he remembered, was one of the ways of dealing with the faerie folk. Most of their senses didn't do well around iron and steel. I guess they're doing some kind of electromagnetic sensing. They could hear some things and make sounds—pretty creepy ones. They don't do their tunneling themselves, they've got some kind of rockworms that do that for them. And their tunneling creates things that look just like natural caverns, complete with the formations. We're not sure yet what they actually want all those minerals for; maybe they eat them or something."

Mamma handed me the secret album, and I flipped to the centerpiece. Jodi sucked in her breath. The things in the picture could be faked by modern technology, but the picture was clearly from twenty, thirty years ago. The thin-looking legs and arms attached to the more massive body were very like Baum's Nomes, while at a distance the head with its mass of crystals atop and fluted tube below could look like something with a head of hair and pointed beard. The crystalline "eyes" were located about where a human's would be, so overall the effect was very bizarrely humanoid, in a creepy way. The thing had a braided crystalline harness around its body, holding what looked like a sword sheath and some other crystal-and-stone accoutrements.

Next to it was a low-slung thing, apparently of the same general order of living creatures by its gray-rock luster, but otherwise unrelated. It was much more reminiscent of centipedes in general construction, but the head glittered with points and tubes and glints of grinding structures. It was a clearly alien thing with an even more alien purpose.

"I took that shot," Mamma said proudly. "Second time down, first time seeing them, never let out a peep."

"Developed it herself too," Father said. "Mamma Bea insisted we get pictures."

"*Oy!*" Jodi shook her head. "So, these things are real. I believe you. So what did you mean 'something like that,' when I asked you that question?"

"The Nomes lost track of Winston when he ran away, and for a while nothing happened. Winston found he could sneak around and spy on them, sometimes, without them noticing. For the next few years Winston didn't go down much, though, because there were the New Madrid Quakes which made anyone going underground awfully nervous. About 1816 he started regular trips again, this time focused on scouting out the Nome territory. Either he got clumsy or they got lucky, but this time they followed him to the exit. They don't seem particularly inclined to violence, but they seemed to want something from him and made a nuisance of themselves for a few days, though they never seemed able to actually approach the homestead."

"After the second time Winston got himself some diamonds, though," Helen continued, "they changed their approach. Even tried to get into the house, though they clearly were almost blind here. Winston found he could bash them senseless with an iron bar and they were almost unable to hit back."

Jodi glanced at me. She'd finally made the connection between my habit of carrying a crowbar and the family history. "So, you've been dropping in on these poor people every few years and stealing their diamonds, and then you have the *chutzpah* to beat them over the head when they object? Have I got this straight, now?"

The family stared at her open-mouthed. While, upon reflection, I agreed with her assessment, I don't think anyone else had ever put it that way before.

Father got his voice back first. "Point," he admitted.

"I'm impressed," she said sarcastically. "And here I'd thought all the eminent domain conquests and oppression of the native population had been finished years ago."

"It wasn't as if they were doing anything with the stones, girl!" Grandpa objected. "Just leavin' them sit in pools o' water. We had better use for 'em."

"And if someone decided you weren't making use of your furniture, what, you think they could just come in and take it?"

"Hold on, let's not get in a big argument here," I said, to head off an explosion by Grandpa. "For what it's worth, Jodi, I agree with you. I didn't think it through before. So what do you think we should do?"

"Have you geniuses ever thought of talking to them?"

"Not recently," I admitted. "But several times people have tried to communicate. They don't seem to be able to see writing the way we do, and admittedly both sides are either mad or scared whenever they meet, which doesn't dispose them towards expending lots of effort to understand us. On our side, well, if they've got a language we haven't noticed it yet. They carry some things that look like tools, but darned if anyone's ever seen them making one, so we don't even know how they do things in their civilization."

Jodi frowned. "Well, it's a *furblungit* mess, I'll say that. But Clint, you tell me: is that picture one of an animal or a person?"

"Person," I said without hesitation.

"Well, then?"

The family was silent for a long moment. Then Grandpa heaved a long sigh. "Girl, you have a tongue for sure, and I don't know whether I envy Clint now. But damn-all, I guess you're right. Can't keep going down there takin' a man's stuff without even askin'. Even if the man's made of stone."

Jodi failed miserably to hide a look of superior triumph. "So you'll go return this last batch, right? Maybe that will start a communication going with them!"

We winced, and Adam bit his lip. "Um, Jodi? Can't rightly do that. Don't have them any more."

"What?"

"Most of 'em are already sold. We kept some as a reserve, but given the way they work it's not like we're gonna try to hide 'em in the cellar. They're in the safety deposit down to the bank."

She grabbed my keys off the table. "Okay, then, Clint, let's head on down to the bank and make that withdrawal."

There was a distant rumble of thunder. I opened the door, expecting to see clouds, but the sky was clear blue. "What in— ?"

Then I saw the cloud of gray-brown dust rising from the trees. "Father!" I started running towards the forest. Jodi and the rest of the family followed.

I skidded to a halt a hundred yards into the forest. "Holy Mother!"

The prior damage to the road had been nothing. A yawning pit over a hundred feet wide dropped straight into the earth, edges surrounded somehow by upthrust rock that formed a barrier that even my truck would never pass. It would take weeks to make a new way around.

Grandpa came puffing up behind everyone else, his bum leg having slowed him up. "Kids! Kids! Get back to the house now!" He caught sight of the hole in the mountainside and cursed. "Listen!"

We listened. The forest was as silent as a grave.

Then we heard faint, deliberate movement. Heading towards us.

Slades aren't cowards, but we're not stupid either. The Nomes couldn't drop the homestead, sitting on that massive, unsuspected foundation of nickel-iron, but they could take the ground where we stood out from under us. And they were aboveground, in force, in the daytime.

"Something about this last raid," I said, "seems to have really pissed them off!"

"Never done this before?" Jodi asked.

"Nothing on this scale," said Mamma Bea, handing Jodi a length of steel bar.

As we rounded the bend towards the gate, something burst from the underbrush, a shining stone weapon leveled at Jodi, screeching like a berserk set of rusty springs running over potholes. In bright daylight, there was little human about it—sparkling crystals on its head, faintly fluorescent violet eye-crystals, and that howling screech from the tube in its face which made me and Father jump back.

Jodi didn't even flinch. Her steel bar parried the stone sword and carried it around in a disarming arc that sent the weapon spinning away.

"What, don't get pushy with me! I've seen taxi drivers scarier than you!" Her New York accent was strong enough to cut, the only sign of how scared she really was. Jodi poked her bar in its stony chest, making it shrink back in disorientation, holding its arms up defensively. "Back off!"

It stumbled backward, bumping into another one that had belatedly decided to try to back up its buddy. We took advantage of the delay to make it through the gate and lock it.

"Power on, boy!" shouted Grandpa.

"Way ahead of you, Grandpa!" Jonah shouted, outsprinting me as he streaked towards the house. We saw a dozen—two dozen—gray figures at the fence, pulling at it. Strong and well fastened as we'd made it, I could see that they'd be through it in minutes.

Then tearing-metal shrieks echoed from stone throats and the Nomes leapt away from the now-electrified fence. A few of them shook weapons in our direction, but I swore that I heard a note, not of fury, pain, or anger, but desperation in the voices.

Voices?

We all collapsed to the ground, catching our breath. Finally I turned to Jodi. "It looks like we go to Plan B."

She drew a very shaky breath. "Okay, yeah, we're now surrounded, the road's gone, and they're waving sharp stone things at us. Let's do that Plan B." She looked at me. "Just what *is* Plan B?"

"Talk to them," I said, grinning. "I think we just might be able to do it now."

6. VOICES OF THE EARTH

"**T**ell me again just how this is supposed to work, Clint?"

I should have expected Mamma to ask again. I was never sure how much of her cluelessness was an act and how much was sincere lack of understanding. I compiled the subroutine, tested it with the main one, started running it on some test data. "It's what I do, Mamma. Signal processing is, well, it's teaching a machine to do some of the same stuff that we do naturally. If you figure out how, sometimes you can eventually get the machine to do it better than we do."

She continued making sandwiches for Jodi and me. "Can you give an example your silly mother could understand, dear?"

"You're not silly, Mamma." I thought for a minute. "Okay, try this. There's a big party here, everyone making a lot of noise. Evangeline spills hot water on herself and gives a holler. Do you think you'd notice?"

"Well, sure enough I would! Don't you think I could tell when one of my own children might be in trouble?"

"I know you could, Mamma. That's what we can do with our built-in signal processing. You've got twenty voices, all making a ton of noise, but somehow our brains can sort out the different voices and notice when one specific voice is doing something unusual, like shouting in pain, even if the actual volume in the room should, by rights, be drowning that voice out."

She nodded slowly. "Never thought of it that way, but you're right. A mother can hear even a small sound by her baby over a powerful lot of noise."

"Right. So we can program a computer to do that, too, if we know how to tell it the tricks of the trade. Turns out there's a lot of different ways to do that.

"For what we're doing, the important thing is that there's different kinds of sound, what we call frequencies; high-frequency sound's high-pitched, low-frequency's low-pitched. I had a project I was on, once, that had to sort out human voices that were whispering at a distance of, oh, about three hundred yards. The kinds of signals I got from that looked a lot like some of the ones I was getting from Jodi's sensors, except that these were up in frequencies you only see bats screeching on. So I'm guessing the Nomes talk way up out of our hearing range. This converter setup will shift ultrasonic frequencies down to our range, and kick ours up to the ultrasonic."

"And I hope you've got everything set, because I don't think our neighbors are going to wait much longer." Jodi set down the heavy packs.

"Got everything?"

"Steel weapons in case they stay hostile, three sources of light—caver's lamps, flashlights, candles and matches—radio relays, walkie-talkies, food, clothing change, rope and climbing gear, hey, you name it, plus the stuff we cobbled together out of our gear. This isn't the first of these hikes I've been on, you know. Just that this *mishigas* changes some of the extras we need to bring. You got the code for our little universal translators, Geordie?"

"Mr. Scott, please. You know Next Gen was a weak, pale imitation. Yeah, the code should work. It's not all that complex and I could adapt a lot of the code I already had. But it ain't really a translator, remember; we're not going to understand them." I took two smooth alloy cases in rubberized jackets from her. "Oh, that's right, we already had some of these set up for long-term monitoring."

"What else could I use? We don't know how long we'll be out or where we'll be, so it's a good thing we had ruggedized, sealed cases for this kind of thing." Jodi was right—in the cave environment we expected, the gadgets we brought had darn well better be awfully tough.

"I've got the code just about set. You've got extra battery packs?"

She patted me on the shoulder. "Hey, have a little faith in your techie fiancée, *neh*? I pirated all the batteries from our stuff. Taking no chances."

She glanced over at the rest of the family. "I admit, all the gadgets you people have not only surprised me, they'll come in handy. Wouldn't have expected you to have short-range radio repeaters."

Grandpa laughed. "Hain't much difference twixt this adventure of yours and some of the ones we've thought 'bout doing over the years. Never had to use 'em yet, but Adam durn near did for this last trip. If most of us come with you an' provide relays with our own radios, those relays should take y'all a good long ways in before we gets out of contact."

Radio, of course, would be attenuated real fast through all that water-soaked rock, but relays could really stretch that, especially if we used the family to stretch it farther. Evangeline, Grandpa, Mamma, and Helen would be staying topside; the rest would follow us down. We knew the Nomes hadn't—and couldn't—come up through the Slade entrance, not with all the iron around and below the entrance. The only question was whether they'd try to kill us when we got out of that area.

DIAMONDS ARE FOREVER

I transferred the code into our equipment and spoke into it. There was a faint sideband of whining high-pitched noise, but the instruments showed most of the output centered around the same waveband as the signals I thought were the Nomes' voices. I put the outdoor headphones on and walked out into the night, pointing a parabolic mike in the direction of the besieging force.

"*Choura mon tosetta. Megni om den kai zom tazela ku*," I heard, or something very much like that. The voice was tenor, with an odd, scraping quality to it.

"*Zom moran! Zettamakata vos bin turano*," replied another, deeper voice. Chills went down my spine. It was one thing to have figured it out intellectually, another to actually hear the voices of nonhuman creatures. I pulled the headphones off and turned back. "I was right. Voices. Damn!"

Jodi nodded. "Didn't have any doubt myself, love."

Jodi and I each clipped one of the little boxes that contained the signal processors, memory, and whatnot that did the conversion to our belts, ran compact headphone wires up inside our clothing, and put on the slim-profile headphones that fit under our caving helmets. No one goes caving with a bare head, unless they want to end up with lumps or worse. We tested all the connections, made sure all the power packs and other gadgets—repeaters, lights, and so on—were well distributed, and then turned towards the door. "Let's do it. Time's getting short. They've started testing the fence again."

I led, Jodi followed, with Father, Jonah, Nellie, Adam, and Grandpa bringing up the rear. In the darkness the huge grating seemed even more grim and forbidding, and opening it was like watching a mouth opening up in the earth. We turned on our lights, checked all our equipment again, and descended the iron ladder set into the living rock; as agreed, Grandpa stayed topside to keep the exit secure, just in case, and to be the topside relay.

It's a long, solemn climb at the best of times; the iron ladder drops straight down into pitch blackness that first muffles the sounds of the outside and then starts amplifying the echoes of your descent into a cadence of solemnly echoing drumbeats. Ninety feet down, my feet touched stone. I looked around, saw nothing in the immediate vicinity, and stepped away to let everyone else get down. The sounds of people and equipment echoed through the tomblike silence of Winston's Cave, silence normally only broken by water dripping from the ceiling.

"Okay. Everyone ready?"

"Ayup," Father answered. "Nellie?"

"Yes, Father. I'm first relay. I'll be right here at the base of the ladder." She took out her iron truncheon, swung it around, and leaned back against the iron ladder. We heard her checking reception with Grandpa topside as we moved down the Snake's Belly, a twisting passageway with scalloping where swift-moving water had carved it out. The lights glinted brightly off water-slick rock, giving back highlights of yellow, brown, and white

64

from the flowstone that coated parts of the wall. We moved cautiously, waiting to make sure we could see as far ahead as possible.

A flash of light ahead. I stopped, then turned one of our Mag-Lites on and aimed it down the corridor.

Across the tunnel, just where the Snake's Belly exited into the Crossroads, five Nomes stood, weapons aimed at us, rockworms waiting at their feet. By now, only Adam and Father were with us, Jonah having stayed back about halfway down the Belly because the signal was starting to fade. We'd probably have to leave Adam at the beginning of the Crossroads. I took a deep breath. "Guess this is it."

I put on the headphones; Jodi did the same. We walked forward, Father and Adam following some distance back. As we approached, I heard *"Turano! Turano zom ku!"* in a sort of whispered voice, and the figures tightened their grip on their weapons.

When we were within twenty feet, I stopped. My heart was pounding awfully fast, and for a minute I couldn't convince my hands to let go of my trusty iron bar. At this range, in this light, the Nomes and their rockworms were too eerie to contemplate for long. I forced my grip to relax and handed the weapon to Jodi, then took another slow couple of steps forward. They muttered something and gathered themselves. Something about the tone of voice and the way they almost bunched together actually heartened me. Why, they were afraid of us too!

"We don't want to fight you," I said, the microphone taking my normal voice and catapulting its sound to seventy-five thousand cycles higher.

The reaction was everything I could have hoped for. They literally jumped backward in startlement, and I couldn't even sort out separate word-sounds from the gabble of Nome-talk that erupted from the headphones. Finally they settled down and one of them stepped slightly forward, stone sword still in his hand but lowered to a much less threatening position. "*Rennka ku? Mondu okh wendasa hottai rennka?*"

I shrugged. "Hey, I don't understand you, but I get the idea you're surprised I talk. We just found out that you did ourselves." I reached very carefully inside one of my pockets and took out a small bag. I put the bag down on the ground and backed up a few paces to where Jodi waited.

Whatever senses they had, they'd been able to tell I did something there, at any rate. The spokesman came hesitantly forward and stopped, staring at the bag with his weird crystal eyes. Then his face snapped up, looking at me with a very human startlement visible in his pose despite the stony immobility of his features. "*H'adamant! H'adamant huran zom!*"

Jodi and I looked at each other, startled. "Adamant?"

It clapped fists together in what was somehow an exultant or agreeing motion. "*H'adamant! H'adamant!*" It scooped up the bag and emptied the three diamonds into its palm—last of Winston Slade's original cache, saved for sentimental reasons in our safe—and held the palm out to us. "*H'adamant, vu!*"

"I'll be damned," I said. "Wonder if they got that word from us, or we got it from them?"

Jodi shrugged. "Don't have any idea. But he looks like he's coming down from his ecstasy."

Indeed, the spokesman was now looking in his palm, and loosed a steady stream of words which included "*H'adamant*" as a frequent occurrence.

"Sorry, sir, but we don't have any more of them." I tried gestures to get the point across. "Maybe we can reach some kind of understanding?"

He finally seemed to realize no more diamonds were forthcoming. He then pointed down the corridor—clearly, whatever senses they had must have some analogy to sight, at least when used for that purpose—and made emphatic motions that I couldn't interpret as anything except "Come with us."

"Well, it's what we wanted," I said, not feeling all that comfortable with the idea.

"So long as what they want isn't to cut us open to see if we have the rocks inside us."

"You just had to bring that idea up, didn't you?"

"Clint. Best get along now."

"Yes, Father." We started following the Nomes. Adam stayed behind at the beginning of the Crossroads. When we reached the entrance to the Corkscrew, Father knew he would have to stay behind also. He gave me an unexpected hug. "Be careful."

"We will, Father."

The Nomes talked with themselves in low undertones. They'd clearly realized we didn't understand them, and at this point had stopped trying to talk to us. We followed farther into the bowels of the earth. After a while, I keyed in the radio. "Father?"

The Nomes and the rockworms spun around at that, staring at me again.

"Hear you, son. Getting faint. Figure a few dozen more yards."

The Nomes relaxed slowly, then continued on, but they were now talking with great intensity and animation. "Something about the radio really set them off."

Jodi nodded. "Well, makes sense, doesn't it? You said they must sense things in the electromagnetic, and that's why the iron throws them off. That radio might be like a flashbulb or something to them."

I dropped one of the relays. The rearmost Nome stopped, turned, and came back towards us. It picked up the relay. I stepped towards it, it backed up, studied the relay for a moment, then put it back down and glanced at me. I let it move away and then continued walking.

Soon we were entering areas of the cave that even Winston had never seen, past the Hall of Mysteries and obviously deep into what was the Nomes' territory. Now I really started to get worried. We were seeing other Nomes around us, who would stop and point and start to gabble amongst each other, just as prisoners being marched through a city would start to see the citizens point and whisper.

There were only two of our eight relays left. We were now in an immense cavern that I couldn't even see across. The Mag-Lite hinted at its great expanse, reaching the roof overhead, bearded with stalactites that were twenty feet long or more and still ended with well over a hundred feet of air between them and the ground. When we lowered the light it touched on more wonders: gargantuan columns, dozens of tunnel openings, flowstone curtains that glittered translucently, a shaggy forest of helictites beneath a high-up opening that obviously vented air into this area.

Since the cavern was effectively open air, we wouldn't need a relay until we were all the way across it. As we reached the far side, surrounded by the eerie rusty-gate hissing and screeching that was the audible-edge component of the Nomes' speech, something massive came slowly into view. We slowed down and stared for a moment in awe.

If we'd had any remaining doubt that this was a civilized species, we would have lost it then. For the first time we saw an undeniably artificial construct in the depths of Winston's Cave. Towering before us, over sixty feet high, were a pair of what could be nothing but titanic doors. In a way they still seemed to belong here, their surface as smooth yet naturally flowing as the rest of the caverns. They were composed of what looked like marble, but with strange, almost interwoven components of a semitransparent black stone which looked like obsidian. They were covered with shimmering alien symbols that appeared to have been grown there as a natural part of the stone. We could not grasp what the symbols meant, though they were clearly the work of intelligence.

None of our guides made any attempt to open the door. There was a sound of rushing water, and the great slabs simply pivoted up and rose smoothly out of sight as we approached; almost noiselessly, without any visible sign of the truly impressive force that must be needed to move. I saw the thickness as I passed . . . four-foot-thick slabs of stone. I did a quick mental calculation. Mother Mary, together those doors must mass over a thousand tons! I dropped the next-to-last relay just outside the doors.

Jodi evidently decided that it was time for a clearer look, because she pulled out the big electric lantern and turned it on.

Beyond the huge doors was . . . the Throne Room.

Even if I hadn't been half expecting it since I was a kid, there was no way I could have called it anything else. The penetrating beam of the portable lantern barely made its way across the room, maybe over a thousand feet in diameter. Circle upon circle of Nomes, each with its weapon and companion rockworm, stood in what looked like a military attention pose, with a narrow gap through which we marched. The great domed cavern sparkled everywhere with the same alien designs. I wondered, vaguely, how they saw such designs, and what they "looked" like to their eyes; surely what we saw was at best only a part of their symbology. In the center of the cavern, a series of concentric terraces were laid, with rough-surfaced ramps curving in a spiral fashion to each level. And at the top of this raised formation, on a perfectly circular polished dais of stone over fifty feet wide, was a throne, hewn from the living rock it sat upon, with a single Nome seated in it.

This was the meeting I'd half dreamed about, half feared for almost twenty years. I couldn't think of *this* Nome as "it." He looked down at us from an elevation of fifteen feet, counting the height of the throne itself. His crystalline crest seemed finer and higher, the fluting on his chin longer, and he looked to me to be somewhat larger than the others around the room, or those escorting us. In the shadowy light of the stupendous throne room, with my overexcited imagination working at double time, I could almost see the halo of white hair and long beard. This was Ruggedo, sometimes called Roquat, the Red—the Nome King.

I shook my head to clear it. I might not be able to keep from giving him the name in my mind, but there wasn't any other connection. This was a first contact between humans and whatever this race really was, and I wouldn't help matters any by letting kids' stories influence my behavior. And whatever they were, they had a lot of things in their civilization that we hadn't the faintest clue about. Behind the throne we could see bizarre and distorted shapes; things that looked like they might have been living things of the same general sort as the Nomes and rockworms, but jammed together, intertwined and almost sculpted in ways that hurt my eyes to look at.

"Father," I said into the radio. "We're about to meet the Nome King."

"Then mind your manners, son."

Ruggedo (as my mind still insisted on calling him, lacking any better name) had leaned forward with interest as I talked with my father. He leaned back slowly and studied us as we were brought up the ramps until we stood before him, a mere twenty feet from the being who was clearly in charge of this entire underground world. His head tilted slightly, as though he were a bird trying to see us with one eye, and then another. Now I could see there was, in fact, one strong similarity between the real and the fictional Nome King: Ruggedo did, indeed, hold a heavy, elaborate scepter with a great glittering red crystal at its end.

"That thing gives me the creeps, Clint." Jodi spoke in an undertone, having wisely shut off her high-frequency transducer.

I just nodded. She wasn't talking about the King, but about the shapes behind the throne which we could now see much more clearly. This was not a good thing. It was something inherently unsettling, seeming a blend of the living and the living rock, shapes almost like attenuated Nomes blending into rockworms and other . . . things of even less familiar outline, like an unholy blending of Bosch and Giger. My earphones hummed and murmured with whispered sounds of the Nome language and with other things, like barely audible whines, interference, and subliminal voices.

We stood there a moment, each side regarding the other in motionless silence, broken only by the sounds that even our transducers couldn't render into recognition. I took the time to study the King closely. Even though he was clearly larger than his subjects, the Nome King still wouldn't stand taller than Evangeline; I guessed him at no more than five feet tall. The body was almost spherical, with variegated geometric patterns of black, green, brown, and yellow making it look almost as though he wore clothing, at least from a distance; up close, it was much more a natural mottling of the skin. Round, slender arms and legs, with rocky sheathing that had the appearance of thin clothing on their bodies, completed the resemblance to Baum's Nomes, as envisioned by John R. Neill. The crystal growths on the head, up close, didn't really bring hair to mind. They shimmered with multiple colors—the King's seemed predominantly violet, amethyst perhaps—and the immobile eyes and stony tube jutting from the chin emphasized the alien nature of the creature.

Finally, the Nome King leaned forward on his scepter and spoke.

"So, *you* are the people who speak in the air!"

7. UNDERGROUND UNDERSTANDINGS

Neither Jodi nor I really know precisely what we did in that moment. That clearly spoken English sentence stunned me so much that all I know for certain is that we stood there for a while, staring at him with our mouths literally hanging open. Just as we started to recover, the King suddenly began to emit a series of whooping noises which, after a moment, we realized must be laughter.

"Hooo Hooo Hooo Hooo! OOOoohoohooohoo! You really do appear that way! Pardon, I mean, look like that—when surprised."

"You speak English?!" I finally got out, rattled enough to slide into dialect. "What th' hell's goin' on here? Weren't four hours ago I first heard a word of your language, an' from their reactions I'd thought was the first time y'all had heard ours!"

That sent him into another fit of laughter. Jodi and I exchanged glances. This wasn't even vaguely what we'd expected. It didn't help that I actually recognized the voice. Well, not really recognized it, exactly, but I knew I'd heard that voice before many times.

Finally he settled down. "In a way, you are quite right. And in another way, no, I do not speak your language. That"—he gestured to the twisted structure behind him—"speaks your language, through me."

That brought all sorts of icky possibilities to mind, just looking at the thing.

"Are you the ruler here, or is it?"

The shrieking snort seemed equal parts amusement and annoyance. "I am the High Spirit here. That is a . . ." He seemed at a loss, finally saying, "*makatdireskovi*. There are several words in your language which seem to partly apply, none of them actually meaning what I am trying to say."

"So what do you mean by saying you hadn't heard our language before?" Jodi asked.

"Never before have we heard your voices speaking in our manner," the Nome King—well, High Spirit—said. "But there were those of us who ventured into *Tennatu*—the Land of Fast Changes—who, in past cycles, began to *turan* certain signals which we realized were not natural. We made this *makatdireskovi* to help us understand what we sensed, and eventually did. But we never realized it was your people who were doing the speaking."

DIAMONDS ARE FOREVER

It took some considerable back-and-forth exchanges before we finally realized that they'd managed, over a period of many years, to derive our language from television broadcasts. That explained the voice—it was a combination of several TV anchormen, most notably Peter Jennings and Tom Brokaw, with a hint of Walter Cronkite. They had realized that part of the transmissions could represent a depiction of objects in some way. But because they didn't see at all the way we did, and within their own "sight" spectrum had a different arrangement of seeing intensities and "colors," they could translate the signal but the "image" they got did not resemble the "image" their regular senses got of us at all. So they had no idea that the babbling in the air came from the same people that sometimes raided their caverns. That was also why it had taken the King several moments to verify that we really did look "surprised" in the same way as the images they had previously extracted from the signals. The *makatdireskovi* and he had needed to find the translation between the signal-images and what he was seeing.

"Okay," I said finally, realizing how much time had passed, "I think we need to at least cover a little business before we go back to this discussion, sir. We came down here to see if we could try to fix up the bad blood that's been built up between us over the years."

He sat still for a moment, head tilting in that birdlike fashion again, and then gave a nod. The gesture was clearly deliberate, something he must have learned from the transmissions they monitored. "I had hoped this was true. You do not seem to be suicidal or hostile, despite the formidable reputation you have among my people. What do you propose?"

"Well, first off, you've got us in your power, so if you'd be so kind as to pull your people back off our land topside, and then I can tell my folks to relax—that we're talkin'?"

He considered that for a moment, then raised his staff and barked out several commands in their own language. "It is done. Tell your people that mine shall bother them no more, at least so long as we remain in council."

I keyed up the mike. "Father?"

He responded instantly, even though it must've been a good hour and a half, maybe two hours of nothing but waiting before he heard anything. "Yes, Clint?"

"We're having a good conversation here and might be here a long time. But we're able to talk together—don't ask me to explain the ins-and-outs right now—and the King has agreed to pull back his people. Can you check that for me?"

"Hold on, son." A few minutes passed, then: "Clint, all disappeared a short time back. Looks like everyone's playing on the level."

I relaxed. The situation could still get bad, but it looked like we were past the worst. "Good, Father. You guys pull back too, then. Me and Jodi can find our way back if we have to, and I don't think we're in any danger here."

"Will do. Be back every few hours to check on you, though."

"Okay, Father. Take care."

"You take care of that girl, hear me?"

"Yes, Father."

"Good luck."

I put the transmitter away. "You know, I think we've forgotten all our manners. I'm Clinton Slade. This is my fiancée, Jodi Goldman."

The Nome King had apparently seen plenty of introduction scenes. He rose up on his slender pipestem legs and gave a low bow. "A pleasure, Mr. Clinton Slade, Miss Jodi Goldman. I am *Rokhasetanamaethetal*, the High Spirit of the *Nowëthada*."

We returned his bow. "Rokasta . . . ?"

"*Rokhasetanamaethetal*," he repeated. Jodi frowned, and I caught the impression of sounds involved in that name that I couldn't even describe.

"I'm not sure I can even say that properly, sir," Jodi said.

"Ah, yes. I recall that the vibrations that formed your language did seem to have, relatively speaking, great simplicity. We can reproduce any such vibration very easily, but you seem to be more limited. Choose another name for me, if you wish. I will see if it suits me."

I was strongly tempted to call him Ruggedo and see if he'd take it, but it was time to drop that line of thinking. "Let's just shorten it a bit, sir. How about Rokhaset?" The name sounded vaguely Egyptian, said that way, and the tube-beard did kinda look like the tight little beards you saw on the Egyptian statues.

"That will do well enough. Come then. You have stood long before my throne, and in the images your people send through the air the *makatdireskovi* has noted that you prefer to sit, as do we if the time is overly long."

He gestured with his great scepter, and the other Nomes parted along the line of the gesture. It was a smooth and well-practiced movement that simultaneously gave me great respect for their attentiveness and reaction time, and a bit of wariness about our so-far genial host. That kind of coordinated, instant obedience I'd only seen in humans when the boss was a pretty hard-assed tyrant . . . or in a very heavily drilled military establishment.

At the far end of this pathway, a passage was visible in the light of our lantern. Noticing the beam again for the first time in a while brought something urgently to mind. "High Spirit, sir?"

"Just call me Rokhaset, as you have named me. Might I call you Clinton Slade and your friend Jodi Goldman, instead of by formal terms? Yes? Very well, then. What is it?" The High Spirit led us down this new course.

"Your people see using senses we don't—I guess the word you're using for it is '*turan*'—and we see using ones you don't. The problem is that our light's going to go out in not too many hours, and we'll really be pretty helpless without it." This was something of an exaggeration, as we had several light sources on us which would enable us to manage some kind of illumination for quite a while, but I wanted to see what his reaction was.

He tilted his head. "Rather as I am *matturan* near you and your iron and steel, eh? Give me this lantern of yours for a moment."

"Be careful with it," Jodi admonished him.

"As though it were a child, I assure you."

Reluctantly she handed him the lantern. He took the hard-plastic-cased giant flashlight and examined it carefully, running his fingers across it. "How do you activate it?"

Jodi indicated the on/off switch, then had to physically place his fingers on it, as he couldn't actually see the gesture. While his people often gave the impression of sight like our own, things like this constantly reminded us that what we were seeing wasn't what they saw.

Rokhaset moved forward. As we went to follow, he stopped and held out a hand. "Wait a moment, please. I wish to be able to examine this clearly, and your presence with all of your iron makes that impossible."

We waited as he moved about thirty yards on, then stopped and examined the light again. There was a click and we were in darkness. "Hey!" I said.

"Just testing. So it is now no longer giving you illumination?"

"It's off."

He verified this by switching it on and off several times, then brought it back to us. "I believe I can arrange something, if I understand the operation correctly." Rokhaset screeched some orders to his people, and then gestured for us to follow. "There are many things for us to discuss, I believe, but first it is time for us to speak together as friends. It has been a very, very long time indeed since my people and yours spoke as one people."

"I wondered about that. There are legends among our people about spirits who live in the earth and who fear the sunlight or who are vulnerable to iron."

"The 'sunlight,' as you call it, merely confuses some of us, and can damage our eyes over time by causing them to fog. There are some beings that avoid your sunlight for more pressing reasons." Rokhaset spoke those words as we passed along a polished-looking corridor. "But I am surprised by your people even having legends, for the time when the *Nowëthada* and the *Tennathada* walked and spoke together is many generations past even for my people. Indeed, it was thought to be no more than legend by many of the *Nowëthada*, as none of them could even tell whether your people spoke at all."

We emerged now into another large hall, but this one seemed oval and had what appeared to be a long table and chairs of odd designs in it, with many Nomes going back and forth. The others formed into an honor guard as we approached. The High Spirit seated himself in the center of one long side of the table, and indicated we were to sit directly opposite him on the other side. The table was about five feet wide, allowing for plenty of room. The chairs were a bit short for us—not unexpected—but after a few minutes of sitting in them seemed surprisingly comfortable, though my legs did feel that they had very little clearance below the top of the table.

"I've been thinking about what you just brought up, Rokhaset," Jodi said finally. "The problem is that there's no way you could have talked with us before. It wasn't until the past, oh, fifty years or so that we could've built gadgets that would let us hear you, and you hear us."

" '*Gadgets*'?" Rokhaset repeated, puzzled. "Gadgets . . . Do you mean these 'machines' like the ones you carry that make your voices sound like ours?"

"Yes."

"Ah. Well, in those days, there was no need of such things. As our legends and histories relate it, we were a much closer people in the ancient time; that is, you and I would have seemed less alien to one another, and we would have had ways of speaking together that would be considerably more simple. But then came the *Makurada Demagon* . . . the, hmm, what would make sense in your language . . . the 'Senseless Shattering'? Ah, no . . . Darkness? Hmmm . . . Perhaps the best expression would be something like 'Plague of Blindness.' But that implies a disease, which this was not; it was a disaster which struck the whole world and affected it in different ways for each of the peoples who then inhabited it. The *Nowëthada* lost contact with *Nowë*, who was sore injured by the *Makurada*, and with your people, and while apart, we changed."

"Who is *Nowë*?"

"You would call *Nowë* our patron deity, god or goddess of the Earth. That is what *Nowëthada* means, the People of *Nowë*. It is at *Nowë*'s will that we exist. We are the servants of the Earth, made to oversee the interaction of the living rock with those other things that live upon it." He sat up a bit straighter. "Ah, tell me how this seems to you."

Light began to fill the room, shining out from several stafflike objects being carried into the room by other Nomes. It was light of a brilliant blue-white color, not exactly what I'd have chosen for lighting; but it saved on batteries and our host had apparently had this whipped together just for us. "That's just great, Rokhaset!"

"You had your people do that up now?" Jodi asked. "Well, I'm impressed. Can I take a look?"

"By all means, Jodi." It was still pretty strange to hear such courteous and very well-spoken English coming out of that unmoving mouth. The only oddity to the sound was a slight hollow resonance, but in this cavern setting it was hardly noticeable.

Jodi studied the twisted stony shaft, which ended in a crystal that produced the light. "How do you turn it on and off?"

"I suppose I could instruct it to turn off, but do you not still require the light?"

"Oh, sure, sure. What do you mean, instruct it? Is this gadget voice-activated?"

Rokhaset tilted his head a few times. "There you are, using these words oddly. Tell me, would you call our pets gadgets?"

"You mean those things we call rockworms? No, they're creatures."

"Then what you hold there is not a gadget either, if I understand you correctly."

Jodi nearly dropped the rod. "Are you saying that this thing is *alive*?"

"As alive as I am," the High Spirit agreed. "Not, I confess, nearly as capable of other activities as I. We grew that very quickly for one purpose only, to make that crystal *hevrat* in the same *gos* as your 'lights' . . . how would that be in your language

. . . hmm . . . Yes, we made it to glow in the same way as your lights do. It provides little for us to sense, but for you it appears to suffice quite well."

I shifted uncomfortably, then glanced down at the chair. "And what about . . ."

I almost got the impression of a broad smile. "Ah, you have noticed that they grow, have you? Yes, certainly! How else could we have chairs that all would be comfortable in, for my people vary in size as do yours?"

Jodi and I exchanged glances. I could see her mind following the same path. We kept getting deceived by the Nome's human-sounding voice and his—or, to be more accurate, the *makatdireskovi*'s—grasp of our language, derived from the past forty years of broadcasts. Clearly we had much in common with the Nomes, and there was no reason we couldn't be friends. But, just as clearly, there were some very, very alien aspects to their civilization. The thought that even the furniture I was sitting on, the lights I was seeing . . . "Is everything here alive?"

Surprisingly, that made Rokhaset pause; almost I could see him frowning in thought. "In a sense, yes . . . but not in the same sense as these things, no. The Earth itself is alive in its own way, but certainly there is a difference between the ordinary stone about us and ourselves, or these chairs or your new lights."

Servant Nomes moved to the High Spirit, and other Nomes came in and seated themselves—leaving a respectful, and possibly fearful, distance between us and their leader. The servants placed several stony bowls, plates, and platters on the table. There was a quick discussion with some glancing at us, which Rokhaset resolved with a gesture. "I presume you have brought at least some of your own food, Mr. Slade, Ms. Goldman? For it is time for me to eat, but I suspect our food is not to your taste."

"We've brought some stuff, yeah."

Five huge covered platters were carried to the table, heavy enough to require two Nomes each, and placed carefully in front of the diners. The one in front of the High Spirit unfolded its top like a flower at his touch.

In the brilliant blue-white glow, the dishes within shimmered with the colors of the rainbow. There were slices of some rich brown and yellow rippled stuff that looked almost like a chocolate and yellow swirled cake, some brilliantly red fruitlike things, some really peculiar transparent sticks, and other things like noodles, puddings, and crumbled croutons.

"Are those . . . rocks?" Jodi asked tentatively.

The High Spirit gave us a deliberate nod. "Properly prepared by the finest chefs, of course."

"How do you cook a rock?"

"Not using the trivial methods shown in your media, if I understand them correctly. Your people lost, in some ways, far more than we in the *Makurada Demagon*."

"So," I said, studying his plate, "What are those? The reds . . . garnets, maybe. The stuff that looked like cake slices at first must be layered limestone—the main rock around here."

"You have an excellent eye for one of your people," Rokhaset said. "Though I am not sure of your first identification, your second is quite correct."

Suddenly Jodi began laughing almost hysterically.

"What's so durn funny?"

She finally got a grip on herself. "You . . . you Slades! And the Nomes! All this time, you big, strong frontiersmen have been sneaking in and robbing the Nomes' pantries! You're nothing but overgrown mice with iron bars!" She went off into another fit of laughter.

I blinked. Now there was a completely humiliating thought. "Is she right, sir? Have we been stealing your caviar—special food or something?"

"In a manner of speaking, yes. I admit to having a fondness for *H'adamant* when I can afford to have some prepared. But I would hardly have sent out a legion of warriors to Tennatu just for my stomach!"

"So why did you send your warriors after the diamonds?"

"Not diamonds—*H'adamant*."

"Same thing."

He shook his head, emphasizing his disagreement by using our own gesture. "Ridiculous. I have seen these 'diamonds' in your television advertisements. They are nothing like *H'adamant*."

"We weren't anything like what y'all got out of those broadcasts either," I pointed out. "There, Jodi's got herself a big diamond on her hand, you tell me that ain't the same thing."

Jodi held out her engagement ring. Rokhaset studied it for a few minutes, then slowly raised his head and gazed at us with those weird crystal eyes for a long time in silence. Finally he reached out and placed one of the stones we'd returned to the Nomes on the table between us. "I return your question, Clinton Slade. You tell me that these two things *are* the same."

"Shoot, I know they are. I've studied geology for years, and hell, it ain't hard to tell a diamond. Jodi's ring was cut from one of the ones we got down here."

He stood bolt upright and shrieked out something that I couldn't make out because the transducer's volume cutoff killed it. Jodi and I jumped back, fumbling for the iron bars, sure that we were about to get mobbed.

But no one else moved in a way that seemed hostile. If anything, they huddled together a bit more. Finally Rokhaset got himself under control. He sat down slowly and selected another morsel off the plate. I could see now that the mouth was located under the sound-tube he used for speaking—sort of where the chin-neck juncture would be in a human. He didn't seem to eat this with enthusiasm, but more like a man doing something while thinking.

Finally he looked back at us. "I must beg your pardon. It is hard for someone such as myself to suddenly realize how alien your people are. I had foolishly permitted myself to think that because your words are translated to ones I understand by the *makatdireskovi* that we are really essentially the same, aside from a few minor differences." I got the impression of a long, shaky breath being drawn, though all I could see was a faint movement of the stony skin on the rounded torso. "To give you something you might understand, telling me that the . . . stone in the ring that Ms. Goldman is wearing is the same as this *H'adamant* would be the same as my holding out one of your skeletons and telling you, in all seriousness, that I could not tell the difference between the skeleton and the living, breathing *Tennathada* before me."

He shuddered, a movement rather similar to our own. "Your people have lost more than I had ever imagined. This"— he indicated the natural diamond—"is a living stone, Clinton Slade, Jodi Goldman. The *H'adamant* is precious because of that living essence within it. Now that I know your people cannot see the difference, and that you call both by the name 'diamond' . . ." He shook his head again. "What a terrible waste. You cannot even see what it is that you destroy by cutting the stone in the way you do. We had foolishly thought that you needed the . . . diamonds for the same reasons we did, for their special properties."

"Well, since we're on the subject," I said, after a moment's pause, "we'd like to come to a more peaceable arrangement. Maybe a trade, something you'd like for stuff we'd like. Maybe we can bring you stones like aren't around here?"

Rokhaset nodded thoughtfully. "Yes, there are ossibilities—many crystals and minerals that we know of, yet cannot find here. But we would have to give you some way of making sure you brought us live stones, not ones whose essence had been damaged or destroyed. However, there are more pressing matters. You returned these few stones as a gesture of your goodwill, and so I have accepted it. But it is essential that you return the ones you took recently."

I shifted in my living chair. "Well, sir, we can't exactly do that. For two reasons."

"That would be extremely unfortunate. What reasons are these?"

"Well, firstly, your people kinda wrecked our road. Really bad, this time. It'll take a week, at least, before we have a chance of getting out of here and making it to the bank where we keep the stones."

Rokhaset's eyes flickered—literally—but the tone of his voice was warm and perhaps slightly amused, so I guessed that the flicker might be something like a smile. "What the *Nowëthada* can destroy, the *Nowëthada* can rebuild, and just as swiftly, Clinton Slade. If that is all that stands between us and the *H'adamant*, lay your fears to rest."

I sighed. "Sorry, sir, but that's the smaller problem. Y'see, most of them are already sold. We've got some left, but not even a tenth of what was took."

The whole room seemed to go silent. Rokhaset sat utterly immobile, as did the other Nomes, and for a few minutes it looked like we were stuck in some lunatic sculptor's workshop, surrounded by macabre statues.

When the silence broke, it was by a hurricane of sound, gabbling Nomish voices all talking at once, with one alien word repeated so often as to be recognizable even in the Babel of noise: *lurizata.* The Nomes had risen from their seats and were now shouting back and forth at each other, sometimes gesturing unsettlingly in our direction.

Just as it reached a new crescendo, Rokhaset's voice boomed out: "*RATCHOTAI!*"

Dead silence fell again. It only lasted a split second, however, because the quiet was instantly broken by the High Spirit talking to his people. Well, I say "talking," but it sounded more like a lecture—or a tongue-lashing. He laid into them but good. We couldn't understand it, of course, but we could pick out "*lurizata,*" "*H'adamant,*" and some of the other words we'd heard before. His people shrank back, just like humans getting bawled out by the boss, as he continued his tirade. It must've lasted a full five minutes before he stopped, seemed to take a breath, and turned back to us.

"My apologies, Clinton Slade, Jodi Goldman. Your news is very disheartening, and it seems some of my people were unready for such bad news. We had always believed you kept the *H'adamant* on your property. With all the *H'kuraden* that underlies it, we could not of course sense the crystals at any distance to see if they were in fact there. I should have realized the truth once I understood the diamonds of your transmissions were what became of our *H'adamant*. Unlike some of my less courageous subjects, however, I refuse to view the situation as hopelessly lost."

"I think," Jodi said, "it's about time you told us just what the real problem is, *neh*? What's so vital about this particular batch of diamonds that you've just got to have them?"

The High Spirit looked over at her, then gave one of his deliberate nods. "Yes, you are correct. But let us finish our meal first. A few more minutes should make little difference, and the story is long and not entirely pleasant."

I was never so anxious for a meal to be over.

Eric Flint and Ryk E. Spoor

8. ASSAULT OF THE EARTH

"Ours," began Rokhaset, "is not the only city of the *Nowëthada* in the Earth."

We were seated in another set of chairs, which were slowly adjusting to become more comfortable in their creepy way, in a smaller and obviously more private room, a circular cave about thirty feet across and twenty high, hung with hundreds of delicate straw stalactites dripping water on most of the area; we'd pointedly stood near the two dry spots in the room and waited for the Nomes to move the chairs for us. While we were getting seated, I'd finally asked Rokhaset why he was excluding the other Nomes, which seemed to amuse him.

"Few of my subjects can hear what the *makatdireskovi* sings to me, Clint. It was designed for me alone. Therefore, any with us cannot understand you, nor speak to you, and would thus be of little use in our deliberations. The only reason they understood some of what we discussed while dining is that one of those who can, somewhat, hear the *makatdireskovi* was summarizing what he heard, something as one of your reporters or sports announcers. This would be somewhere between clumsy and useless at this point in our discussion. Now that it has become clear that the signals involved are important we shall have to make something which will speak to—or perhaps to be more accurate, translate for—all our people as the *makatdireskovi* does to me. But that is a project far more complex than simply making you lights." This relieved me to some extent. Rokhaset didn't seem to be the tyrant type, although military leader still seemed likely.

"Yes," Jodi said, returning to the subject, "I wouldn't expect you were the only city."

"The problem is that the *Nowëthada* are no longer the unified race we were. Those who survived the *Makurada Demagon* . . . all of us changed. But some changed more than others. Our task was always one of balancing the way of the Earth with the way of the life on its surface. But as we became less like you, and the powers of *Nowë* faded, the old senses which used to tell us how to perform this duty also weakened and faded." He rubbed his hands, a gesture which seemed like a slow shaking of the head. "To allow your form of life to survive and prosper, of course, it was always important that the world remain overall peaceful. But changes must happen to the world as well, and so it was our job to ensure that these changes were sufficient for the world's purposes, and to minimize the injury to people such as yourself. This task we continue to this day."

I could not help but be tremendously impressed by the *makatdireskovi*'s work. Oh, now I could understand how it was possible; the thing was a living construct, probably with the brainpower of a hundred Nomes but all focused on the single task of translating. Still, the way it was taking two separate languages and even apparently conveying accurate nuances of emotion . . . hell, there are career actors who can't handle that job in their own language!

"Like all spirits, however, we had our opposites, those charged with the release of destructive impulses from the Earth, the eradication of other life through disasters, and so on. While *Nowë* was active, both sides had the great Senses that told us when each approach was correct or incorrect. And so we cooperated with each other and with your people in ensuring that the great dance of *Nowë* was carried out properly. Over the span of millennia, however, that was lost, and the *Lisharithada* were changed horribly by the *Makurada Demagon* into a race of creatures who enjoyed the destruction they could create and sought ways to make it worse, if possible."

"So you're at war with them, then?" I asked.

Rokhaset began another of those sudden shrieks, but cut it off. His voice was heavy with sadness when he continued. "War? By *Nowë*'s heart, never! We try to negate their efforts. We are made to cooperate, to assist, Clinton Slade. Killing and fighting is tremendously hard for us. We have warriors, yes, and they are formidable in their own way. But they do not kill except in self-defense or by accident, even such creatures as yourself. Kill our own people? It is not even to be imagined easily."

"So you try to sabotage their efforts, sorta undoing their work, but you can't fight them directly?"

"In most cases, yes. We can directly fight them, in small numbers, under very specific circumstances—when what they are trying to do is of sufficient destructive scale that it is not merely our lives, but those of countless others involved. It is then that we truly need the *H'adamant*."

"For . . . ?" Jodi prompted.

"In your language, I suppose the best term would be 'potion' or 'elixir.' Your own people understand certain symbolisms with *H'adamant*, now that I realize you call them by the name 'diamond.' The basic symbolism is not far from correct. If the Earth wills it, we can extract the essence of *H'adamant* and preserve it in an elixir which will make us stronger in virtually all ways—more capable of withstanding injury, and quicker, physically and mentally. In this way we are able to utilize small numbers of our people to oppose their vastly larger forces, to cut through their defenses, and to neutralize the rituals in which they invoke such massive powers of destruction."

"They can fight you, right?"

Rokhaset nodded deliberately. "Oh, yes, Jodi Goldman. Enough of our old instinctive accord survives that even they will not attack us for no reason—there will be no genocide here, despite our opposition. But if we are actually intruding on their territory and interfering with their work, they most assuredly will fight us, and can and will kill our people. As you can see, this places us at a grave disadvantage without *H'adamant.*"

"Okay, I get you. And right now they're planning one of their big parties, right?"

"One which, if you will pardon the use of one of your own idioms, will assuredly bring down the house." Rokhaset seemed grim. "And for the second time, your people, Clinton Slade, have made it impossible for us to stop it . . . and both your people and mine will pay the price."

"Second time?" Now, I was getting really nervous, as I started to get a glimmer of the horror that was waiting behind Rokhaset's account.

"Second time, Clinton Slade. When your ancestor first entered our caverns and stole our entire cache, cloaked by the *H'kuraden* he carried, he did so at the worst possible moment; the times and powers had aligned so that the *Lisharithada* could carry out one of their greatest destructive rituals, and suddenly we were powerless to stop it. For a time we believed that somehow they had found a way to bypass the mystical defenses that surrounded our most secure caches. It was almost a relief

99

when the next theft's source was traced to your forefather. But that did not repair the damage from the first theft. For a while, we had convinced them to moderate their behavior, but then your people truly began your intrusions upon the Earth, and their anger grew. Now the same forces have aligned once more, and the *Lisharithada* prepare to unleash them with even more fury than they did a short time after your ancestor had robbed us for the first time."

"Holy Mother of God." I heard myself whisper, unable to stop myself. "You're talking about the New Madrid Earthquakes!"

What Jodi said at that point I can't repeat. Rokhaset simply bowed his head.

"Look, Rokhaset, we gotta try to stop 'em at least! We'll head topside and you guys will help us get the road back, so's we can get you the diamonds that're left. We could try to buy some more back."

Rokhaset nodded. "We shall try, Clinton Slade. We shall hope the *H'adamant* you still have shall suffice, but I have grave doubts. We do not have the time for you to buy some more, I am afraid. To make the elixir will take two and a half days, as you measure time. They will strike in four days, as that is when the forces will be at their peak of alignment. Do you truly believe you shall be able to locate so many *H'adamant*, arrange for their purchase, and deliver them to us, in time for us to make the elixir and then carry the battle to them? Even as things are, it will be difficult, leaving aside the fact that, as your people do not know or respect *H'adamant* for what it is, there would be no way of telling whether the ones you purchased retained their true virtue until they had actually arrived."

There wasn't any arguing that. Four days . . .

I tried not to think about it, but anyone in my profession has already visualized the consequences of a Richter 8+ quake east of the Mississippi, and the New Madrid fault has always been the chief suspect. The area of effect of a major quake in this area would be monstrous: ten, fifteen times that of a comparable quake on the West Coast. It would level almost everything manmade in at least three or four states, cause heavy damage in adjoining ones, and be felt from the Rockies all the way to Vermont, maybe even Maine.

"Waitaminnit!" I said, suddenly thinking of something. "These *Lisharithada*, they live underground like you do, right? Well, if they set off a Richter eight quake right here, what's gonna keep 'em—and you, for all of that—from being squished when the quake brings the caverns down?"

"We are spirits of the Earth, Clint. We have our ways of preventing our own homes from breaking. Unfortunately, this is not true of your homes, or of caverns which we no longer inhabit."

I stood up. "Well, sir, seems to me we've both got work to do. We need to get topside so's we can get the *H'adamant* back, and you'll need to get your people to rebuild our road."

"Indeed." He stood as well and after a moment offered his hand, another gesture he had clearly been shown by the *makatdireskovi*. I took it; the skin was cool and hard, like shaking the hand of a rough-hewn statue, but no statue ever squeezed back that way. "Clinton Slade, Jodi Goldman, it has been a pleasure, truly. I regret we have met in these circumstances, yet perhaps *Nowë* shall smile upon us and somehow we shall stop the coming disaster." He shook Jodi's hand as well. "Shall I send an escort with you?"

"No offense, sir, but you people don't seem to be the fastest sorts. I remember the route, and I think me and Jodi can make it back a lot quicker on our own."

Jodi nodded. The route was long, but it was actually pretty direct, and we had blazed our way with more than just dropped relays whenever there was a doubtful intersection.

"As you will. My people can move quickly, but not for long distances. There you have the advantage of us."

* * *

We left the throne room with hundreds of Nomes lining our path, holding their weapons in a very different manner.

Clearly the word had spread that there was now an accord between us, and they were expressing their understanding as clearly as they could without their ruler's peculiar advantage.

Once out of the throne room, we made time, pushing as fast as safety would allow. "Father, I don't know if anyone's listening, but we're on our way out."

"Clint!" came Jonah's voice. "Y'all okay?"

"We're fine, and the Nomes are right nice folks, but we've got ourselves a powerful lot of trouble. Tell you about it once we're up."

Jonah said he'd get the family, so I signed off. The next four days were sure going to be interesting, but like in the old Chinese proverb way.

Eric Flint and Ryk E. Spoor

9. TOO LITTLE. TOO LATE?

"We might be 'bout four days from Armageddon, or leastwise that's how it's going to seem around here," I started out.

The whole family was gathered around the table this time, from Evangeline through Helen and Adam on through Grandpa.

"But you said the Nomes isn't our enemies, right, Clint?" Mamma asked anxiously.

"Right, Mamma. But it turns out they've got relatives of their own that there's a feud with. These boys play on a bigger scale than we ever figured, and we Slades have gummed up the works but bad." Jodi and I went on to summarize what Rokhaset had told us. "So unless we can do something to help 'em out, in four days the New Madrid's going to cut loose with a Big One and ain't nothing going to be left standin' for hundreds of miles, least of all the Slade homestead."

The family sat there in silence. It was an awful lot to take in at once. And somehow it sounded a lot more fantastic here, in the comfortable electric lights of the family room, than it had in the blue-white glow of Rokhaset's domain.

"You think they can do that?" Father said finally.

I exchanged glances with Jodi. "It's hard to say, Father. But . . . yes, I guess I have to believe it. What reason would they have to concoct such a silly story if they had a more reasonable motive for wanting the diamonds? We sure didn't show any sign of needing anything that outlandish."

"Well," Evangeline pointed out, "y'all did say they learned how to talk with us from listenin' to the TV and radio. Lord only knows what they think is normal, Clint."

I chuckled despite my worries. "You got a point there, Evvie. Jodi?"

She tossed her dark hair back, then shook her head. "I think Rokhaset's pretty clear on how we think. No way he'd waste his time making up some *bobbe maisse* like that one; he's got more important stuff to do."

"Well, then, we give 'em all the diamonds we have left and hope it's enough." Mamma said.

"Do more than hope, Mamma. Pray. If this doesn't work, those destructive cousins of the Nomes are going to cause the biggest disaster the States have ever seen."

"What can we do, Clint?" Adam demanded.

106

"Grab our tools and get out there for when they start trying to get the road back. It's easy enough to wreck something, but they don't drive cars, and I'm not sure they'll know what has to be done to really make it driveable. And shut off the fence. They're not going to come after us now that they know us." I felt my eyes trying to shut. "But me and Jodi have to get some rest."

"Lord, of course you do," Mamma said. "Why, it's been almost twenty-four hours you've been up, and most of that either hiking the caves or facing Mr. Rokhaset, which must have been about as scary as anything!"

"Get up to bed," Father agreed. "Need your strength later."

Jodi and I didn't argue. We knew there wasn't any way we were staying awake much longer. I stumbled up to bed, feeling my feet get heavier with every step. The clothes I peeled off seemed to be made of lead, and I don't really remember hitting the mattress.

✻ ✻ ✻

I woke up with a hoarse shout, as the ground quivered underneath the house. "*JODI!*"

"A *CHORBN!*" I heard the Yiddish curse echo all the way down the hall. "*What?* Did they move up the schedule?"

By then, I was out of bed and down the hall, bursting through Jodi's door. The shaking was already over. "No, no, that was just a little one. But Holy Mother, did that scare me!"

"And I was calm, you think? *Oy!*" She was still in the bed, nude from the waist up since the sheets had slid down when she sat up abruptly. The view was on the spectacular side. Her long, curly, lustrous black hair was spilling over her shoulders, framing her chest. Jodi was basically a slender woman, but not everywhere. I was a little transfixed, for a moment. Memories . . .

She looked me up and down, suddenly grinning. "You look as nice as I remember, too, *neshomeleh*. But you might want to put some clothes on before your family decides *we* caused all that shaking and bouncing around."

I looked down. I was nude from the soles of my feet up.

"Oops. Hey, look, I was startled. Gimme a second."

By the time I got back to her room, with my bathrobe on, Jodi was already out of bed and wearing her own robe. In that respect, if nothing else, she certainly didn't fit the stereotype of a Jewish-American Princess. Jodi was always punctual and could get dressed faster than a fireman. How she manages that, I'll never know, because the end result was never sloppy. Every item of clothing was on right, buttons square, zippers zipped, hair brushed, the works. Even the many times I'd watched her do it, I'd never really been able to figure out her secret. She just seemed to pour herself into her clothes, shoes and all—hell, *work boots* and all—and she had the kind of magic hair that, despite its length and thickness, immediately fell into place at the touch of her fingers.

When I walked in, she was muttering something to the effect that the much-vaunted stability of the nation's conservative inner regions compared to decadent Manhattan was obviously a be-damned lie. About a third of the words were in Yiddish so I didn't catch all of it. But the last phrase came through clear as a bell: "—least the *ground* doesn't mug you!"

"C'mon," I chided, "what's the big deal?" I imitated her accent. " 'The trucks on Fifth shake my apartment harder than that!' "

She giggled despite herself. "Okay, wisenheimer, you'll get yours. But only after I get a shower."

We both needed showers badly after the last day. If I hadn't been so dog-tired I'd have showered before going to sleep, but collapsing in a shower isn't the best idea.

So, half an hour later, we met downstairs. A frustrating half hour, since Jodi and I like to take showers together which maybe accounts for why we usually take such long ones. I was finding this *be-proper-before-the-family* routine was getting old really fast. Even the prospect of continental catastrophe in four days wasn't enough to squelch all my normal *I-want-Jodi* enthusiasms.

I guess I muttered something to that effect. "Stop whining, Clint," Jodi instructed me, as we headed for the kitchen. "Look at it this way. Soon enough we'll either be dead or we'll be married and either way you won't have to worry about it any more. Getting laid, I mean. You'll still have to scrub my back—don't think for a moment I'll let you off the hook on that just 'cause you're my husband. Or a corpse."

Her stern and stoic words would have been more effective if she hadn't goosed me as I started through the kitchen door.

Mamma was in the kitchen, looking exhausted herself, but with enough food to feed four of me laid out. "Nice to see both of you up, Clint dear, Jodi. Father and Adam are up to the road, along with Helen and Evangeline. Everyone else just went to bed, which is where I'm going now."

"How's it going up there?"

She gave a tired smile. "Lord, they're devilish looking things, but those rockworms and their keepers can work miracles. We just might get this done in time, Clint. Might could. Best eat up and go see for yourselves."

I gave Mamma a hug, which she returned—a little tighter than usual. She kissed Jodi on the cheek and then headed upstairs. I turned to the table and dug in.

"We slept ten hours, Clint. Down to three and a half days or less now. We have to get into town, get back with the diamonds in less than a day."

I nodded, wolfing down some ham. "I know, I know. Let's get up to the road, see what they're up to."

It wasn't a long hike, and in the sunlight it was less eerie, though no less strange, to see the hurrying pipestem-limbed Nomes and their centipedal assistants. As we came to the edge of the huge scar in the earth, I sucked in my breath. Buttresses of limestone were forming, curving in rippling bands to create supports for the stone that would lie atop them. It was the rockworms which were doing most of the work, chewing up rock in one place and depositing it, changed and molded, in another. I looked around and saw Adam, Father, and Rokhaset under a large spreading oak at the far edge.

We hiked around to them. Looking down, I could see that the rockworms came in differing sizes, from the little ones about two feet long up to one nightmare-inducing monster nearly twenty feet long, with horns and spikes of crystal adorning its head and a mouth that looked more like a rock-crusher than anything living.

"Father, Adam, Rokhaset." I said in greeting.

"It is good to see you again, Clinton Slade, Jodi Goldman," Rokhaset acknowledged us.

"Clint. Jodi. Work's going."

"And fast, too," Adam said. "Their . . . what was the name again, sir?"

111

"*Seradatho H'a min*, or you might call them simply *seradatho* for short."

"*Seradatho*, yep, they just make the rock as we stand here. Ain't maybe as fast as a full construction crew, but it's plenty fast enough. I think."

"Is it safe for me to go down and look?"

Rokhaset gave a deliberately human shrug. "The *seradatho* will not harm you on purpose, Clint. But some may not notice you immediately, even with their handlers present, so take care."

I slid down into the pit and walked carefully up to one of the medium-sized *seradatho*, which was starting to put some kind of joining stone between some of the buttresses. I examined the resulting stone carefully, then climbed back up. "Sir, that looks just like standard cavern limestone! I swear, if I took that back to a lab I wouldn't be able to tell the difference!"

"And nor should you. We are part of the Earth, Clint. How many times must I say this before you truly understand? Nothing that we do may be apart from her. Except in our own dwellings, it must not even be recognizable as our work, but be fully in harmony with *Nowë*, as much a part of her as we are."

I shook my head, still trying to comprehend it. "But it looks like standard flowstone—deposited over thousands and thousands of years. How the hell can you possibly replicate that?"

"I could attempt to explain it," Rokhaset said, after some consideration, "but in truth, without taking much time indeed to instruct you, all that I could tell you would boil down to saying 'it's magic,' a most unsatisfactory explanation. Suffice to say that this is the way it must be for us."

"So some of those natural-seeming caverns we see around the world are really your doing?"

"Undoubtedly. Sometimes your people intrude upon us by exploring what you think are natural caves and are, instead, our dwelling places. Only in the great cities and central places of the Earth do we build places such as the throne room and its nearby environs."

I rubbed my temples. Running into the Nomes themselves, well, I'd always known they were there. So it was more like just meeting some aliens. This, though, was magic—a kind of magic that affected stuff I really did know a lot about, and direct enough to hit me in the gut. The threat of the *Lisharithada*'s great quake was real enough, but too huge to grasp, really. Seeing stone that, by rights, ought to have taken a million years to form be spat out in seconds by some crawling centipede-thing, that was different.

I remembered, suddenly, the rushing water I'd heard when the great doors to the Throne Room opened. "You don't even use machines like we do. You just channel water and maybe use levers or something to move those doors and other things."

"Correct. In nature, sometimes water does move great boulders, so we can construct a device that takes advantage of that."

"Well, Clint, now we know why we've never seen any traces of these things before in caves around the world."

I nodded to Jodi. "Ayup. We *did* see traces, more'n likely. Problem is that there was no way to tell the traces from the original stone. Y'all even make stalactites and stalagmites and all the trimmings, right, and make sure the water's there to keep it alive?"

Rokhaset seemed pleased that I'd picked up on the last part. "Exactly right, Clint. I see you have finally penetrated the significance of your original ancestor's find."

"In a cave, water flowing represents life to you just like to us. So you keep your diamonds and other stones in those pools so they stay a part of *Nowe*'s essence, right?"

"Very good. Yes, precisely so."

I noticed Rokhaset was staying carefully in the deepest shadows under the tree, and remembered his prior comments. "Hey, you said your eyes might suffer in the sun. I could get you something that probably will help."

"Indeed?"

"Yeah. I've done some work with multispectral optics, off and on, and you mentioned your eyes get messed up slowly. I'll bet the crystals are being affected by the ultraviolet rays, which you'll never run into underground." I handed him a pair of UV-blocker sunglasses.

He put them on and glanced around with his odd sight. "Extraordinary. There is minor interference from these glasses in how well I *turan*, but I can tell that the faint pain from the light here is considerably lessened."

"I wasn't sure if the plastic would interfere with your own senses, but the fact that it blocked UV made it worth a try. UV's generally the culprit in most damage sunlight does."

"I believe you are correct in this case. Thank you." Rokhaset glanced into the pit. "I do not suppose you have a few dozen pairs of these?"

I chuckled ruefully. "Nope, and can't get any until we get to town."

"Then let us arrange that as swiftly as possible."

✳ ✳ ✳

The next few hours passed quickly. Rokhaset drove his people and their seradatho twice as hard, pausing only to listen when we clarified how the terrain would have to run in order to permit the cars to pass. Before our eyes, the landscape healed; it was the only way to describe that incredible sight. Stone and soil literally growing up out of the bowels of the Earth, a foundation of limestone covered by soil, and trees and brush somehow moving in over the scar through careful manipulation of the soil and roots.

Finally, the hillside was solid again. "Now, Clinton Slade, it is time for you to fulfill your part of this bargain."

"I'm on it. C'mon, Jodi, we've got a withdrawal to do up to the bank, and darn little time to do it in. We've gotta get to town in less than an hour or the bank will close!"

We dashed to the truck and got in. "Strap in tight, Jodi— y'all's in for a hell of a ride!"

Fountaining gravel, we pulled out of the gateway and thundered downhill, plowing over the newly-laid earth and leaving its first set of tire tracks. The new road around the first gash slowed me down some, being as it had to make a sharp curve, but I opened her up again and had all four wheels off the ground at the first drop on the straightaway. We jolted against the harnesses and even with the heavy shocks she nearly bottomed out. "*Oy*, Clint, slow down! We can't make any withdrawals if we're dead!"

"Ain't no slowin' down, sweetheart. If'n you remember when we drove through last time, takes all of an hour and ten minutes to get to town. And we can't take that long nohow."

"Your accent's getting worse, Clint."

"Yeah, I know. It's 'cause o' th'truck," I said stoutly. "A pickup jest naturally brings out th' inner hillbilly in a man."

Pavement, albeit pretty crappy, was now under the wheels and I opened her up as much as I dared. There's places where you can make over 70, and others where even a nutcase wouldn't go past 30 on those roads, unless he was stone drunk. I drove like a stone-drunk nutcase and Jodi just hung on to the doorframe and said nasty words in Yiddish.

We came screaming down the main street with me riding the brake to get down below the limit as we passed the town line; I think Sheriff McCloskey almost lit off his lights before he saw it was me. I skidded us into a spot in the parking lot and jumped out for the doors, just as I heard the soft but final *click* of the bank door being locked for the day.

"Son of a—" I couldn't quite stop in time to keep from whomping the doors. Arlene Ebsen, the manager, gave me a stern look, but turned around. "Clinton Jefferson Slade, I've known you since you were in diapers, and I know your mamma raised you better'n that!"

"Sorry, Miss Arlene, really sorry, but I've just gotta get into the deposit vault. Please!"

She pursed her lips. "Clint, you know we like the Slades as our customers, but I can't just go openin' and closin' at someone else's convenience."

"*Please*, Miss Arlene, I'm beggin' you. I'm right here on my knees, I mean it." And I was. We just couldn't miss it by this much, we just couldn't!

She rolled her eyes. "Well, Lord, if it's *that* all-fired important . . . just this once. But don't try this again!"

The sound of the door unlocking was like the whole weight of my truck lifting off my back. "Hurry up, y'hear?" Arlene said. "That there vault's on a time lock. Locks itself down in half an hour after closing, less'n someone's in it, but if someone is in it, it screams fit to wake the dead."

"Don't you worry!" I said, racing ahead of her, key already out. "Be gone so fast you'll think I wasn't even here."

Jodi waited back by the doors. After Arlene took my key, matched it with hers and opened the safety deposit box, she marched out of the vault heading for the phone. She was probably going to call Father to make sure there wasn't some reason I might be trying to make off with the family treasures in secret. It didn't take me long to get out the diamonds, since they weren't loose but stashed in three little bags. I slammed the box shut again, locked it hastily, and hurried out of the vault towards the outside door. Passing Arlene, who was just hanging up with a slightly bemused expression, I said: "Thanks a million, Miss Arlene!"

I took a bit more time on the drive back. It'd be awfully stupid to get us both killed now that we actually had the diamonds Rokhaset needed and weren't racing against a specific deadline. But it wasn't easy, because my foot kept wanting to hammer the gas, and from her expression I think Jodi felt the same way. We were going to be in good time overall, but still, it felt like every second counted. It was getting dark by the time we made it back to the homestead. I parked the truck and jogged to the front door.

I then faced what might have been the oddest sight I'd ever seen in my life: Rokhaset was sitting at Mamma's big table, everyone else eating her cooking and him with slices of some kind of stone on his plate, as though he was no stranger a dinner guest than some new neighbor. Strange, yeah, but I felt a huge swell of pride in my family. Okay, so we Slades had been barbarians to these people, but damned if you could call us barbarians now. I wouldn't bet that one in a thousand families could have a Nome at the table and treat it—him—like proper company.

Rokhaset stood as we entered. "The *H'adamant*—do you have it?"

"Right here. Hope it's still alive, like you call it."

As I put the bags in his hand, he nodded. "I can hear it. Weakened slightly by time away from the heart of *Nowë*, but still there." He fumbled with the bags a bit, examining what was inside; he didn't need to open them. I wasn't an expert in Nome body language, but it seemed to me he slumped a bit.

"My thanks to you for a valiant effort, Clinton Slade," he said finally. "But it is as I feared. There is not enough here—not nearly enough—to provide us with a force to overcome what the *Lisharithada* will have to defend them. We shall do our best, of course; it is our calling and destiny. But we shall never triumph."

I stared at Rokhaset. "No. We can't let it end like that."

"Of course we can't, Clint dear. And we won't," Mamma said tartly. "Mr. Rokhaset, we've come invisibly into your homes and taken your diamonds; it's about time we made it up to you. How do you think a few Slades might change the odds, down there in your little war?"

The High Spirit turned around to face her. "You would fight for us?"

"Well, it's for my family too, isn't it? And it's our fault, as Jodi showed us. Now, I only married into the Slades, but what I was taught was that a Slade admits when he's wrong and fixes it until it's right."

"And that's the God's honest truth," Grandpa said forcefully. "Damn this bum leg! I'd come if I could, but I'd slow y'all down."

"Only a few," Father said. "Not like Nomes; can't live without light, need lots of spares."

"I'm going," I said.

"And so am I." At the reaction of the others, Jodi snorted. "What? You think I'm not tough enough? I've lived in New York for years, that's more than tough enough to take care of some *shlemiels* who think they can just start an earthquake whenever they want to. I'm tough enough to keep Clint here in line. You just try me."

Debate in this argument wasn't going to last long. We knew we had to field a pretty strong team, but a lot of the family had to stay behind, both because of the limits on equipment and because if we failed, the rest of the family had to stay behind to get everything out of the house and save as much of the homestead as possible when the Big One hit. So it was me, Jodi, Father, and Adam.

Rokhaset nodded slowly. "It may work. Never in all these centuries have your people helped us, and with your ability to use the *H'kuraden* as both weapon and cloak . . . yes, it could be enough. I—"

He froze suddenly. I was puzzled for a moment, then realized that he must be getting news through the same kind of link he had with the *makatdireskovi*. A few moments later, he looked back at us, and I could tell just by the way he stood that it wasn't good news.

"It appears that the *Lisharithada* want to make sure we are not able to interfere." Rokhaset sat down slowly. "They have deliberately sealed off *Nowëmosdet* between our area and theirs. While we can, especially with the power of *H'adamant*, pass through, they will doubtless have forces waiting there to slow and harass us. There is no way that a *Tennathada* could possibly reach them."

The room that had been optimistic a moment ago now seemed utterly sunk in gloom. After a few moments in silence, Rokhaset forced himself to his feet. "I must take the *H'adamant* to my people. It may not suffice, but I must at least make the attempt, and none of my people can come here to fetch it. It requires quite extraordinary efforts by myself and the *makatdireskovi* to maintain my communication at all. Others of my people would be crippled in the attempt. Farewell, Clinton Slade, Jodi Goldman, and all of your kin."

Something was nagging at me as he left, but it refused to gel. The door closed.

Grandpa slammed a hand on the table so hard it upset three glasses. "Damnation! So close!"

Mamma sighed. "I suppose we shall have to prepare for the worst now. If only there was another way."

Suddenly it clicked. *Another way!* I raced out the door. "Rokhaset! Wait!"

He turned, a dark shadow with faintly glowing eyes. "What is it, Clint?"

"Listen, some people have had a theory for a while now that most if not all of the caverns in this state, maybe farther, are connected somehow. Would you know if that's true?"

He nodded. "It is true, Clinton Slade, though finding the connections could be difficult for your people, and not all connections are direct. Why?"

"Then we come at them from a different direction, if you can tell us the right route to take! Mammoth Caves, Rokhaset— if there's a route through there, we can hit 'em from behind!"

He stood very still for a moment. "It is possible. Barely possible, Clinton Slade, for the route shall be long even if I can find such a route that you can pass, but . . . it is worth a try. Get out all the information you have on these 'Mammoth Caves' while I deliver the *H'adamant*. I shall return and we will see if, perhaps, there is one last chance for us all."

10. PAGING ARNE SAKNUSSEMM . . .

"**I** *really* don't know about this," I found myself saying for the twentieth time.

Rokhaset waved a hand at me to be quiet, so I shut off the transducer that bounced my voice into his range and turned to Jodi. "I meant Mammoth Caves as an example, I guess. I mean, look how far away it is. You know how long it takes to get through anything except a tourist section of a cave—a lot of the time you wouldn't measure things as miles per hour, but more like hours per mile. Or hours per hundred yards, in really hairy terrain."

Jodi nodded. "But Rokhaset has some idea of what we're able to handle, I'm sure. He's not *narish*. Maybe he knows something we don't and that's why he asked for more maps."

"Maybe. But I think I'd best make sure." I got up and went over to where the High Spirit was standing, seeming to look into thin air, and turned the transducer back on. "Rokhaset—"

"A few more moments, Clinton Slade, and then I will answer your questions."

Rokhaset was actually looking at our maps, which hadn't been easy to arrange. Once more, the fact that the *makatdireskovi* allowed us to talk as though we both actually understood each other's language had tripped us up. We'd gathered all the info we had on Mammoth and other, more nearby, caves, only to realize—the next day, when he arrived—that Rokhaset could neither see the pictures and diagrams nor read the words on paper. It had taken a couple hours of panicked discussion, and then a few more of hours of jury-rigging by Jodi, to arrive at a solution. But with the help of an old video camera and some low-power broadcast kit-bashing, Jodi had made it possible for Rokhaset to receive images of the books and maps in the same way they had been intercepting transmissions all along. Another hour had been required to help Rokhaset interpret the diagrams in a way analogous to our own so that he could then try to coordinate what he was seeing with what his people knew about the underground world. Now the High Spirit was trying to put together what he knew with what we knew and see if there was, indeed, any chance of us reaching the *Lisharithada*'s domain in time via another route.

A few moments later he turned. "I believe it can be done."

"Are you sure?" I asked. "No offense, sir, but you gotta remember that we're surface people, and makin' our way through underground passages takes time. Hell, that's something like a hundred miles from here. Even topside I'm not sure we could cover that distance on foot, an' that's straight-line distance, which ain't what you're dealin' with underground."

He made a weird sound I interpreted as laughter. "True and more than true, Clinton Slade; and yet it can be done, I think, though it shall be far from easy." He turned to Jodi, who was testing connections on her latest improvisation. "Are you ready, Jodi Goldman?"

"Try it, Rokhaset. If you can duplicate the transmission pattern, we should be set."

Given the manner in which Rokhaset and the *makatdireskovi* communicated, and the fact that the *makatdireskovi* received and interpreted TV and radio broadcasts, Jodi had wondered if it could, through Rokhaset, replicate the transmission in the other direction. After some consulting with the semisentient geobiomystical device and his advisors, Rokhaset had announced that it should in fact be possible; if so, he would have an ideal way of communicating the chosen route to us.

For a moment, the TV in the room just showed wavering patterns of static. Then, so suddenly we jumped, a test pattern and sound appeared, just like on any standard broadcast station. Except, of course, this was on one of the channels that shouldn't show anything but dead air.

I swore I could almost see Rokhaset grin. "Ah, so it works. Excellent. Then I can show you and you can record this into your portable computers."

We hooked our laptops up through the RF modulator and checked to make sure the signal was being recorded. "Let 'er rip, Rokhaset."

A map of Kentucky appeared, with purple highlighting the Slade homestead and bright green marking Mammoth Caves. The highlighting was shaped like an octagon instead of a circle, the way we usually do it, but aside from that and Rokhaset's apparent preference for using our colors in painful ways, it looked just like one we would produce.

A bright red dot came into view, looking to be somewhere in Muhlenberg County. "The *Lisharithada* are based here, very nearly halfway between the great cavern complex you call Mammoth Caves and our own homes. You must disrupt their operations here in order to prevent the ritual from being carried out.

"Now, I fully realize the distances involved, and if you indeed had to travel in the normal fashion through ordinary caverns, there would be no way for this to work. However, one of the reasons both we and the *Lisharithada* have remained in this area for so many ages is simply that more remnants of the Old Ways have survived here than in nearly any other part of the world. One of these remnants is a portion of *Nowëmosdet.*"

I remembered the word from earlier, but I'd presumed it was just a term for cavern. "What's that?"

"You might call it '*Nowë*'s Road,' I suppose. In the old days there were many interconnected tunnels, like cities, and passage between them was made easier by a sort of network of canals invested with *Nowë*'s power—the *Nowëmosdet*. Two long segments of it still exist in this area. One connects our area with that of the *Lisharithada*, and this is of course what they have closed off to make it difficult to traverse. The other section was traditionally used only by the *Lisharithada* as it goes in the other direction. It is ironic, in a way."

Jodi and I looked at each other. "What do you mean?"

"One could say that it is the *Nowëmosdet* that is responsible for our current emergency. You will recall that I did not question you as to what 'Mammoth Cave' was; this is because I am all too familiar with that system of caverns, at least in general. While the *Lisharithada* are, as I have described, now very hostile towards your people, the thing that finally pushed them into action is that your people's exploration of the great cave system is fast approaching the point where you might discover *Nowëmosdet*, which would be potentially disastrous even though you could not normally use it as we would. No matter how natural looking, your people would become curious about a straight-line cavern so long and even in design, and would quickly arrive at the *Lisharithada*'s domain. Thus, despite the fact that parts of what you call Mammoth Cave are of historic significance to us, the *Lisharithada* have determined that they will destroy it all to prevent your continued intrusions."

"And just incidentally kill thousands—maybe tens or hundreds of thousands—of us along with it. Nice people."

Rokhaset gave a humming sound that carried the same force and tone as a sigh. "Once they were. In some ways, they are still very much like us. But without *Nowë*'s guidance . . . No matter." The image zoomed in, showing the network of caverns that made up the longest, if not the deepest, cave system known to man, a duplicate of one of the maps we'd shown him. Suddenly, an entirely new network of caverns spread across the map, filling in areas never explored by humans, extending across most of the state and beyond into every area that had stone to support caves—and some, near as I could tell, into areas that normally shouldn't have caves at all.

Rokhaset didn't need to tell us where *Nowë*'s Road was. Even without his highlighting it was sharply obvious, a geometrically perfect line running from near the intersection of Flint and Mammoth's networks directly to the west-northwest almost half the distance to the homestead. It terminated in another tangle of caverns, and then started again on the other side to end somewhere below our feet.

"As you can see," Rokhaset said, "if you can reach *Nowëmosdet*, you will be able to proceed straight to the realm of the *Lisharithada*. Taking into account your size and what I have been able to deduce of your abilities, I here trace the path you must take to reach the Road of *Nowë*."

We watched as the route started at the Historic Entrance, following the route for the now-defunct Echo River tour through the Rotunda and the Historic Tour route to River Hall before diverting to pick up the River Styx and the Echo River. Then it suddenly jagged off towards the connection to Flint Ridge, which was near the middle of Cascade Hall.

"Wait up there," Jodi said. "Looks like the connection that leads to the Road is more over to the Flint side, Rokhaset. Why come in through Mammoth?"

"Two reasons, Jodi Goldman. Firstly, if I am not mistaken, Mammoth is more open and will permit you to make better time in all likelihood, even if you must approach over a somewhat longer route. Secondly, the approach from the Mammoth direction will make it easier for you to reach the tunnel here, which is unexplored by your people and eventually leads you to *Nowëmosdet*. This tunnel will be found at the very top of the chamber. While maps such as this are terribly inadequate for showing elevation, on the Flint side you would be ascending quite steeply before you even reach the level of this known passage. And then you would have a further difficult climb to reach the critical tunnel."

"Whee. Abandoning the tour in mid-stride. That'll liven up the tour, sure 'nuff."

"Get ourselves banned from the cave too. Oh, well, not much we can do about that, *nu*? Just remember to have everything packed and move fast. It'd be embarrassing to have the whole state devastated because we were too slow and some well-meaning tourists caught us." She studied the map. "Still, I don't want to be a *nudje*, but that stretch of *Nowëmosdet* is like to be forty miles long. And filled with water. What, you think we're fish? We're not doing that in two days, that's for sure."

The High Spirit nodded. "I understand this completely. There is a way to give you the endurance and speed needed. But it may not be entirely safe."

"*Give* us endurance and speed? How—" I broke off, staring at him. "Are y'all out of your mind? I don't doubt the stuff works on your people, but it's prob'ly pure poison to us! 'Sides, y'all need it, right?"

"You are quick in grasping the idea, Clinton Slade. Yet you are not entirely correct. The elixir, made according to the ancient recipes, is said to have been the same for your people as well as my own. It is born of the power of the world that sustains us both." He shifted his stance slightly. "It is true that the Powers have changed, so there may be some difference in effect, which is why I say there may be some risk. Yet I sincerely believe it shall produce the requisite effect, and, most importantly, surround you with the aura of one who belongs in the Earth, so that *Nowëmosdet* will accept you and assist you."

"And the fact that you won't have time to make it before we have to leave—which will have to be in very few hours, to be honest—and that y'all need it for your people?"

"If you can be of assistance at all, Clinton Slade, it will be because one of your people, wielding *H'kuraden* and striking from invisibility, will be worth many of my warriors combined. But the true drawback is this: I have but two elixirs at this time, for as you have so correctly noted we shall need far more time to finish making any from your own *H'adamant*. So only two of you may go, and no more."

"That's gonna be me and Jodi, then," I said, before she could say anything.

She looked surprised. Pleased, but surprised. "Hey, look," I continued, shrugging, "I've given up trying to keep you out of it, Jodi. And to be honest, you're probably better at the caving end of things than anyone else here. Ours is a pretty specialized knowledge of how to rob Nomes, not explore caves. That was Winston's gig, more or less, and he's been dead quite a stretch."

"Well, what do you know. Maybe you can be domesticated after all," Jodi said smugly.

Ignoring the gibe, I turned back to Rokhaset. "Okay, let's say we get there. Where, exactly, do we go in this area they obviously control, and what'll we be fighting? How many, what's their weaknesses, that kind of thing. Jodi's done some fencing, as one of your warriors found out, and I'm not too bad in a scrap, but we still probably ain't going to be taking on a whole army at once."

"In the main, their troops will be very much like our own in appearance, but more willing to inflict injury. Still, they have avoided your people over the years, while we have grown used to you. They will be very disoriented by the fact that you cannot be sensed easily, if at all, with *H'kuraden*, and you have advantages of reach and height which, in the caverns they favor, you will be able to exploit."

He fingered the Egyptian beardlike tube on his chin. "Your goal, as I mentioned earlier, is to disrupt their ritual. You must work your way inward along this path from *Nowëmosdet*; in one way this route works in our favor, as the center of their mystic workings is located considerably closer to this branch of *Nowëmosdet*. Once there, you must shatter all crystalline items you see with your iron. This will completely negate the ritual and their power will be broken for many years to come, in which period perhaps we shall, together, find some means of returning sanity to *Nowë*'s realm. It is of course possible that they can overwhelm you if you are slow or unfortunate, but I think you have an excellent chance. The only thing that might stop you . . ." He trailed off, evidently having thought of something quite unpleasant.

"Go on, might as well know the worst."

"The *Lisharithada*, Jodi Goldman, like ourselves, are capable of *wëseraka*—life-shaping, causing the life of the Earth to take the form which best suits our purposes. Alas, in this as in all other things they have turned their power to destruction. They have developed the *seradatho* into efficient creatures of war. Most of these will still pose little greater threat to you than their masters; many of their offensive abilities are designed to deal with our people, not yours. However, if by bad fortune you encounter a *Magon . . .*"

"If we do, how will we know?"

Rokhaset gave one of his eerie laughs. "I assure you, Clinton Slade, you will know. A *seradatho H'a magon* is more than twice the size of the greatest of the *seradatho* you saw rebuilding the road, and is a being bred purely for destruction. It can strike us *matturan* at its approach, leaving us helpless before it. Even if its powers cannot directly affect you, it is huge, armored, equipped to tear and break and dissolve. Flee if one approaches."

That was a nasty image. "And why shouldn't we expect one?"

"Because they are extremely difficult to breed, and even more difficult to control, given their temperament and peculiar abilities. I do not believe they have more than one or two *Magon*, and they will almost certainly concentrate these major weapons at the area they expect us to attack, not the opposite direction.

With any luck whatsoever, you should reach the ritual center and destroy it before they could even decide to redeploy the *Magon*, let alone have it reach you."

I winced. "I don't like trustin' to luck. I'm bringin' everything I can."

"We can't bring too much with us, Clint. That's a long hike, with a war at the end."

"Sure 'nuff, but I ain't goin' to a war unarmed. May not be able to smuggle a rifle past the entrance staff, but might could do some other stuff."

Rokhaset shrugged. "I have seen the power of some of your . . . gadgets, Clinton Slade. But the problem will be to have the chance to bring them to bear. Still, if it does not slow you down, there is no harm in bringing whatever you think might aid you." He reached into a pouch in his woven harness and extracted two octagonal crystal vials and a blue crystal, broken in half. "The *mikhsteri H'adamant*—the diamond elixir. Save it until you arrive at the entrance to *Nowëmosdet*, for we do not know how long it will last for a human, in this age of the world."

Jodi and I took a vial each and stowed them away in side pockets of our packs. Rokhaset then handed Jodi the broken crystal. "Keep this with you; it is attuned to its other half, and with it I can follow your progress and time the arrival of my forces to coincide with yours; perhaps we shall even meet in the domain of the *Lisharithada* and see victory together."

"I sure hope so." I shook his stony hand again, then turned to my fiancée. "C'mon, Jodi. Let's do this thing."

Eric Flint and Ryk E. Spoor

11. THREE-HOUR TOUR

"You sure they'll let us take this stuff in?" Jodi asked.

"F'cryin'—Jodi, stop askin' the same question again every few minutes. I wore a pack the last time I went in, no one said nothing."

"Yeah, yeah, I know, but I'm nervous! Me, okay, I'm not carrying anything all that bad except a couple nasty iron bars, but you—*oy*, if you trip—"

"It's not nitroglycerine, Jodi. It won't blow up without the right trigger. I could carve little doggie statues out of it if I wanted to. No one's gonna search me—unless y'all look so nervous that they think there is somethin' wrong, and then we're in big trouble. I got a permit for my gun, so that shouldn't be a problem. Not that I wanna use either if I don't have to, seein' as how big noises in caverns could lead to cave-ins which would ruin our party right quick."

"Right, right."

Leaving had been hurried. We had to pack everything we could fit into a reasonable space—we couldn't afford to draw too much attention—and picking and choosing while arguing with Grandpa, Mamma, and everyone else about why we were going and no one else hadn't been easy. Easier than the goodbyes, though, since none of us knew if we'd see them again. Even Father had gotten pretty choked up, which doesn't happen, and so that'd set me going, which got Jodi to start in, and I guess pretty much everyone ended up with sniffy noses and red eyes before it was all over and we drove off.

Fortunately for our hoped-for future, Jonah had asked what I was going to do about my car. Given that we were planning on violating federal law in breaking off on our own and all that, it would probably be pretty stupid to leave my truck parked overtime in the lot. Father and Adam would be coming after us about an hour later to pick up the truck and bring it home; if we lived through this, we'd come back home with Rokhaset and the others, rather than suddenly show up back at Mammoth anyway.

Mammoth Caves wasn't hard to find, at least. Major parks get good publicity like signs and all, which I appreciated, as it wasn't going to be likely we'd find anything like that down in the caves. In fact, we'd have to move fast through areas we only knew from tour maps and photos at first. While lagging behind might get us the chance to split off from the tour group at the right point, we didn't dare take the chance that someone might catch us. Put bluntly, if someone *did* try to catch us, Jodi and I would have to stop them instead.

The whole situation was really pretty annoying. If this disaster had happened back around 1991, we'd have been able to get right down to Cascade on the tour, but economics and conservation concerns had put an end to that one. At least one thing was in our favor: the past month or so had been pretty dry and the Green River was low. That meant we'd have dry path to run down for most of it before the splashing started. According to what I could gather, we probably wouldn't hit water much over five or six feet, leastwise not in too many places, which was good; not that me and Jodi couldn't swim, but in hiking clothes with packs, that was a different story.

I ran my finger around my neck; it was getting hot in here, even though I had the air conditioner on. We both had wetsuits underneath the hiking clothes. Any serious caver has them, though I'd only needed mine once. The water in caves at this latitude averages down around 55 degrees, and that's more than cold enough to give you hypothermia right quick.

We pulled into the parking lot, found the entrance and schedules, paid our tickets, then had to sit around for twenty nerve-racking minutes as the next tour prepared for departure. No one questioned our packs, which I thought was a near miracle, given that Jodi looked so jumpy. Maybe they just thought she was claustrophobic or something. Finally, the guide called us together and we all started the long hike—down a path, the two of us trying to hide how hot we were getting now while the guide pointed out the occasional squirrel. About the point when I felt like I was getting set to melt, we started down the stairs through the huge, vegetation-fringed opening that yawned darkly to swallow the staircase and us tourists whole: the Historic Entrance to Mammoth Cave.

Despite our hurry, I had to appreciate the sights. Mammoth is a damn impressive place. The Rotunda, a massive hall, opened up before us, and Colin Blair, the guide, began describing the operation that had taken place in the early 1800s to extract saltpeter for gunpowder from the mines. It seemed a bit ironic to me that the operation began somewhere around the time old Winston had grabbed his first big score from the Nomes. I resisted the temptation to ask how the quakes had affected the cave; the last thing Jodi and I needed was to draw attention to ourselves.

After a monologue that seemed, to my stressed psyche, to be hours long, Blair finally turned and began leading us along through Broadway—only to pause almost immediately to describe the Methodist Church. This was a large cavern with a pulpitlike formation which actually had been used as a church in the past. Jodi and I were slowly permitting others to pass us. Eventually we intended to end up at the very back, fall behind, and hopefully make our getaway without anyone noticing until it was too late to catch us.

"Look at that!" Jodi exclaimed.

As we neared Gothic Avenue, one of the weird phenomena Mammoth was famous for had materialized. Within this giant confluence of caverns, a genuine sheet of clouds had formed and was trailing into the Avenue overhead. I pulled out the camera and took a couple of shots; we might be on our way to save the world, but what the heck.

We continued, past the Giant's Coffin, over the yawning mouths of the Sidesaddle and Bottomless Pits, and then through the maze of the Fat Man's Squeeze. By now we were used to the cavern's impressiveness; it was too thoroughly tamed here to continue to carry the impact, and some of the features we had seen in Rokhaset's domain overshadowed it. Now we were approaching the moment of truth. As we passed through the Great Relief Hall, Jodi and I fell back even farther, finally reaching the very tail end of the group. We lagged to look at some of the features in River Hall, then appeared to head towards the group again as Mr. Blair did the usual glance backwards to make sure all his sheep were following him in the direction of Sparks Avenue. He turned the corner, and we slowed down. No one was looking at us.

Jodi turned and walked quickly towards the pathway that led towards the River Styx. A moment later, still with an eye on the tour group continuing on, so did I. Then we both ran lightly down the path until we were out of sight of River Hall.

"Whew!"

"Shh!" Jodi put a finger to her lips. "We're not nearly out of it yet. Sound carries and they can chase us down fast. Keep moving!"

Move we did, heading farther and farther down. But when we got near Cascade Hall we encountered two things: water, which we expected . . . and voices, which we hadn't.

"Clint? What's going on?"

Belatedly, I remembered one of the National Speleological Society articles I'd come across. "Damn, damn, damn. Must be the NSS team that's helping remove all the old stuff left by the tours over the years. Didn't know they were down here now." I was, like Jodi, whispering to keep from being overheard.

"Well, now what, genius?"

"We go forward, what else?"

Go forward we did. Lights ahead of us showed where the team was working; somewhere quite a ways out in the hall. "Maybe we can make it. We have to angle over that way, through the water. Try not to splash."

Jodi put her foot in, winced as the cold hit her clothes and the wetsuit. "Fun, this isn't. The things I do for love."

"Well, and for the sake of all mankind too."

"To heck with mankind!"

"Shh!"

The water got steadily deeper, until we were both hopping on the bottom with our toes to keep our heads above water. So far, though, no one seemed to have noticed anything. I would've crossed my fingers, but I needed everything I had to keep my balance and keep moving forward. The cold prickled on my hands and neck, but at least the wetsuit had now adjusted and was keeping me from really getting chilled.

Halfway there. In the reflected glow of the lights I could make out the entrance to the tunnel that led to the Flint Ridge cave system. We just might make it!

Just as I thought that, my foot found nothing at all under it and I plunged completely underwater, bouncing back up after having hit a pothole that dropped to eight feet. But that had been enough; my ungraceful entry had made a splash even a deaf man would have had a hard time ignoring.

"What?"

"Who's there?"

"What the hell was that?"

Flashlight beams were probing the darkness and sweeping over us.

"Go, Jodi, move it!" I snapped. "No more point in sneakin'."

"Hey, you! Stop! You can't go in there!"

Some of the NSS team were heading in our direction. I found myself standing a bit higher now—a low ridge of rock was under my feet. Good enough. I reached into the top of my pack, unzipped it. "Y'all just go back to what you were doin'. What we're doin' is our business."

"Look, Jack, you can't come down here! Now both of you get back—*holy shit!*"

His lapse into bad language was probably excusable, as I'd just hauled out an old .45, still nice and dry from inside the sealed pack and the Ziploc I'd put it in. "I said, y'all really do want to just go right back to what y'all were doin' and y'all *sure* don't want to follow me."

"Clint?!" hissed Jodi from behind me. "Are you completely *meshuggeh?*"

"C'mon, man, what's the matter with you? There's nothing worth getting out a gun for here!"

I aimed and fired. The thunder of the Colt was like the voice of the Lord telling Moses to get down off the mountain, and a fountain of white water exploded between the two in the lead; one of them jumped back and went under for a moment, while the other just froze. "Maybe y'all are right on that, but ask yourselves if there's anything worth getting shot for here."

"Christ, David, let the fucking lunatic go wherever the hell he wants!" said an older man from further back. "The cops can catch 'em when they come out."

DIAMONDS ARE FOREVER

The NSS people backed off. I grinned, bowed, and followed Jodi into the Flint Ridge connection.

Eric Flint and Ryk E. Spoor

12. THE ROAD OF NOWË

"**O**w!"

This had been a pretty standard refrain for the past couple of hours. The passages were often tight, some so filled with water that there were only a few inches of breathing space between the water and solid rock. I don't normally get claustrophobic, but there were a few moments there where I got the willies thinking of the millions of tons of rock overhead, waiting to fall on us.

This time it was Jodi saying the "Ow!" and I looked up at a view that I was unfortunately way too tired to appreciate, as I was crawling right behind her. "You okay?"

"Just another rock in the way of my head."

"Is it opening up ahead?"

"Looks like it. It should be, from the map we have . . . yes, there it is. Flattening out."

"I say we take a break for lunch. No one's chasing us, that's for sure." We'd been going for a long time, and even if the NSS team had decided to try pursuit later—which I doubted very much—they hadn't been prepared for a long-term caving expedition and would've had to give it up a while back.

Jodi nodded, though I could barely make that out, and a few minutes later we emerged into a room large enough to stand in, with some flat spots to sit down. "Whew. That'll be a relief."

"I'm starved," Jodi admitted, shrugging off her pack and turning. "I—*oy*, Clint, your face!"

I flushed, which probably didn't make me look any better. "Just my dumb feet. Went under again and tried to come up for air a little fast. Which would've been fine if there'd been two feet of air instead of four inches."

"Are you all right? Jeez, you look terrible!"

I didn't really mind Jodi fussing over my face. It probably did look pretty bad, and it actually felt better after she was done cleaning it off, maybe just because it was her doing it. "Thanks, Jodi. Hey, I love you."

That got one of her best smiles. "I love you too, Clint. Hell, you sure know how to show a girl an . . . interesting time."

"We Slades are never boring." I killed the LED-based light I'd been using—sealed, efficient, waterproof—and got out a few candles to light us during the meal. We didn't talk much for a while, seeing as we were both tuckered out. Finally I put away the sandwich wrappers and drink bottles and put the pack back on. "Not too much farther to go, eh?"

"To the *Lisharithada*? A long, long way. To *Nowёmosdet*? A couple more crawls and then we have to make it to the top of a tall, skinny room. After that, we'll be in pure virgin cave for a ways, and then we get to the Road of *Nowё*."

"Let's do it. Either we're past the worst of it, or we'll find out we're completely screwed. But we'll be done with this stuff in any case."

The "tall, skinny room" was the worst of it. We had to ascend nearly forty feet, some of it chimneying. I had to put in some pitons, just to be sure we wouldn't fall. Finally I reached the top.

Blank rock greeted my gaze.

"Shit! There's nothing here!"

Jodi gave a little sound halfway between a sigh and a groan. "There has to be something!"

I shook my head, raised the light higher. Nothing, nothing . . .

Wait. That shadow up on the side didn't seem to move much.

What looked like a shadow was a dark, narrow opening that took us another five minutes to reach. We finally wiggled into it, crawling down a tunnel that Jodi said reminded her of the Gun Barrel in Knox Caverns for about fifty yards. This dropped out into an almost perfectly circular cavern with completely bare walls, with the large scalloping of slow-running water showing on the limestone. At this point I pulled out the laptop and checked the map, because there were three exits from this circular cave. Taking the leftmost one, we entered a chimney that sloped downward and, with water trickling constantly, was utterly treacherous. I backed up, with my white face reflected on the nearby rock, to hammer in several pitons to secure our descent. There was no way we could've made that descent alive otherwise, and I'd been lucky I could even back up when I did.

Fifty feet or more down we finally hit a sloping floor and were able to relax a bit. This tunnel had a small stream running along one side in a channel about three feet deep, and as the rest of the tunnel got lower we started wading through the stream for extra headroom. After a while this degenerated to our having to wriggle through pretty tight, mostly water-filled spaces; believe me, ordinary claustrophobia is nothing compared to the fear you have to fight back when you're hundreds of feet under solid rock, possibly about to get stuck in a water-filled passageway miles from any help. Without warning, I rounded a corner—it was my turn to lead—and dropped over the edge of a small waterfall, plunging into an icy pond over nine feet deep. I heard Jodi splash down about the time I came up and felt the water of that impact douse me again. Fortunately our sealed lights still worked, so we were able to flounder our way to mostly dry rock and get our bearings.

"We've got a ways to go." I said wearily.

Jodi flopped down beside me. "Well, I'm beat. If we don't rest, it won't matter if we get there or not. Time for dinner and some rest."

I couldn't disagree with that, so we took the time, and gave ourselves a few hours' rest. When the electronic whine of the alarm went off, I painfully dragged myself upright, seeing Jodi do the same. My face ached terribly, and from Jodi's expression I knew it must actually look worse now than it had before; bruising often works that way. "Once more unto the breach."

We passed through several caves filled with subtle ornamentation of flowstone and stalactites, waded a shallow underground lake with green water as clear as glass, climbed a twenty-foot chimney, followed a set of narrow crawlways for a long distance, then scrambled up a huge dome and wriggled through a short passage into a winding tunnel just far enough across for us to walk single-file.

With a startling suddenness, the tunnel opened onto a wide, flat shoreline of a watercourse that extended, ruler-straight, as far as our lights could see. *Nowëmosdet* was huge—a great semicircular hallway nearly two hundred feet wide, with even, flat banks about thirty feet wide on either side of the glassy-smooth emerald-glinting water. It felt slightly warmer here, and there was a hint of air moving.

We stared at it for long minutes, our breathing steadying after all the effort we'd gone through. Then I reached into the pocket of my pack. "Guess it's time."

Jodi got out her vial.

We struggled a bit with figuring out just how they opened, but eventually realized they had to be squeezed and then twisted before pulling off. That over, we stared at each other for a moment. Then I shrugged and tossed the elixir down my throat in one swallow.

I immediately regretted that. Not that it felt bad—it was in fact the opposite. The taste of *mikhsteri H'adamant* was like nothing I'd ever tried before, and I tipped the vial back again, letting the last drop of it linger on my tongue. Sweet, cool, sharp, subtle, cold and warm at the same time . . .

"Clint . . ." Jodi's voice held something close to awe. "Your face!"

I touched my face. I could literally feel the scabs falling away, leaving new skin where there had been raw wounds minutes ago. More than that, I felt exhaustion falling away from me as well, as though I had just put down a hundred-pound backpack. I felt I could jump across that entire giant reflecting pool. "Yeee—*ha!* Try it, Jodi, you'll love it! Shoot, now I'll have to see if Rokhaset's got any other goodies like this in his recipes!"

Jodi swallowed her elixir, and now I got to gape. You could literally see the change, the head lifting, eyes shedding their tiredness, cuts and scrapes fading away like bad dreams. Jodi looked more gorgeously alive than she'd ever looked before, worry lines smoothed away, uncertainty lifted. I knew that I must look the same way—confident, happy, and ready for anything.

"*Oy!* I'd start a war to get more of this stuff. I'm surprised you Slades didn't get yourselves killed."

I couldn't help but grin, and stepped forward. We hugged, kissed, then I laughed and spun her around with another whoop. "All *right!* Jodi, let's see what the Road is like!" I jumped off the ledge towards the water two feet below.

And I didn't sink into the water. It supported me, Jodi goggling wide-eyed while I stared back at her. Then, as though a decision had been made, I began to descend, but as though it were transparent quicksand. The feeling was something entirely different, though.

If you were lucky, you had a wonderful, loving mother who was never too busy for you, who always knew the right thing to say whenever you were sad, or scared, or hurt. If you weren't, you probably wished you did. And if you had a mother like that, you might remember a morning or two when you, as a little child, were scared or lonely and crawled into bed when mommy was sleeping. And mommy, even though still asleep, somehow knew you were there, and her arm reached sleepily out and hugged you close, and you knew everything was completely and utterly right with the world, and nothing could hurt you as long as she was there.

That was what *Nowëmosdet* was like. The presence here slept . . . yet She knew us, and somehow we knew Her, and Her Road was ready for us.

Jodi stood next to me in the water, both of us standing on the bottom, our heads just above the surface, and once more we just stared at each other. Then we took a step forward.

It was as though there was no water there at all—except that we seemed to be somehow supported by it. Walking together, we seemed not to walk really, but to float, carried onward by our intent, not by muscles. We didn't really move very fast at all, but it was without effort. No matter how far we traveled this way, we sensed we would arrive completely rested and ready. Even more odd . . . I didn't feel wet. The dirt had washed from us both, yet otherwise we seemed as dry as if we were walking on the bank.

"Rokhaset, you've steered us right so far," I muttered under my breath. "Let's hope this last leg works out the way you planned it too."

We continued on, through the darkness, towards the enemies we had never met . . . yet.

13. STONE AND STEEL

"I just keep noticing weirder and weirder things."

"What is it this time, Clint?"

"Ripples. We're not leaving any."

Jodi looked down, then behind us. "You're right. No wake. Like we're not even here."

I thought a moment. "No, more like we're just a part of the water. The Road is taking us along just like we were part of the flow. Unless we hit something to cause the flow of the water to be upset, there won't be ripples."

"That makes . . . hold it."

"What?"

Jodi's forehead furrowed as she stared ahead. "The echoes. Something's different. I think we might be finally getting to the end."

I glanced at my watch and received a bit of a shock. We'd been following *Nowëmosdet* for nearly ten hours—which seemed to be no more than fifteen minutes or so to me. "I guess so!"

"Shh. They can't hear most of our talk, but some of the high harmonics might get through."

Ahead, the darkness seemed to thicken, then lighten up into the yellow-gray of limestone. The water of *Nowë* 's Road continued on into the wall, through a passage completely filled with water, but we felt the impetus which had carried us along weakening. The water still supported us, but clearly this was the end of the road.

On the right-hand side the walkway opened up into a huge tunnel, and on either side of the tunnel—*Lisharithada*.

They looked very much like the Nomes, but as I studied them, I could see some differences. The crystal crests which served as hair grew in a subtly three-ridged pattern. Their faces were slightly broader and more sharply pointed towards the chin. And they wore stony armor and carried weapons in a much more . . . comfortable fashion than the *Nowëthada*.

I glanced at Jodi, who nodded. We turned towards the bank.

Even as we made the decision, the Road sensed it. We rose up out of the water and found ourselves stepping easily to the stone above, gripping the iron bars which seemed strangely light now.

As we had hoped, the *Lisharithada* seemed as oblivious to our presence as the Nomes had been when first we met. Rokhaset's people had learned ways of sensing us to some extent—maybe, if by no other way, by paying careful attention to pockets of "air" that seemed even emptier than usual—but the *Lisharithada* apparently didn't have knowledge of, or use, such tricks. Anyway, why would they? No human being could possibly come down this far without them knowing it.

Neither Jodi nor I saw any point in conflict when it wasn't needed. Before we passed between them, though, Jodi caught my arm and pulled me back up the walkway some distance. "Check our route."

I nodded, and we got out the portable. Rokhaset's map glowed up at us from the screen. The *Lisharithada* city was large and complex. I carefully compared the version on the screen with the printed version and made a couple annotations to be sure I could tell which ones were supposed to be above the others, tracing the route in highlighter and checking to make sure Jodi agreed with me. Then I shut the machine down again. While so far there was no sign we were being sensed, given how little we knew about their senses I didn't want to take any chances with having more electronic equipment running near them than I had to.

We passed between the two guards, maximizing the distance between us by entering the large corridor directly in the center. After that, though, we moved to one side, figuring that, like most people, the *Lisharithada* wouldn't generally crowd into the side of the corridor unless they had to and therefore wouldn't be likely to bump us.

As we moved onward, this became a very real concern. The tunnel leading from the Road was empty, but soon it joined with another, and there were many of the city's natives using it. The *Lisharithada* were a busy people. Maybe preparing for this destructive ritual demanded a hell of a lot of work, or maybe they just liked to keep busy, but whatever it was, there were dozens—hundreds—of them in the main corridors. It would have been funny if it weren't so deadly serious—watching how we contorted, jumped, and twisted keeping out of the way of hurrying contingents of rock people. Once one of them passed within inches of me and stumbled, barely catching itself before hitting the ground. Its companion helped it up. "*Pokil mondu ku?*"

The fallen one responded with a quick spurt of language that I couldn't catch, but I did get the word *matturan*, which made me hustle out of there. Clearly he'd gone momentarily blind near me, and that was something we definitely didn't want anyone thinking about too much.

Jodi was more worried about their *seradatho*. Some of the creatures were clearly more formidably designed than those of the *Nowëthada*—guard dogs, so to speak, rather than work dogs. It seemed that these *seradatho* also didn't have any clue we were there, but I made a point of tracking their whereabouts more closely as we moved farther inwards.

"So far, so good." I muttered. "We're about halfway there. Maybe we can make it all the way into their inner sanctum without them catching on. Then we can trash the equipment and get the hell out of Dodge."

Jodi shook her head. "I wouldn't bet on it."

Another great cavern opened up before us, this one similar to the one we had seen back in the Nome's area—clearly a living or gathering place, with lots of traffic. It might have been my imagination, but I thought I could see some of the patterns in their movements and the shapes of the natural-stone areas that served them as . . . what, shop stands? Houses, without roofs because of the lack of weather? Offices?

"Y'know, I think I'm seeing better."

"You only noticed already? I'm like to be seeing twice as far as I usually can."

"I just hope this stuff doesn't wear out too soon."

We came into sight of the next intersection. "Aw, shit."

The free ride had evidently come to a halt. Probably the next area belonged to their ruling class. Whatever the reason, this one had a door on it, and the door was guarded by three *Lisharithada*, who were being given a wide berth by the others. Even if the direction they were going would make it sensible to cut close by the doors, the others—civilians, I supposed—would detour quite a distance around instead.

"Can you see how to open the damn thing?"

Jodi and I studied the area for a few minutes. Then she pointed; after a moment, I nodded. Like their less warlike brethren, the *Lisharithada* tried to use natural approaches even to technological problems. There were, barely visible from where we stood, a pair of channels in the stone floor where water could run down and into holes in the wall. The channels actually connected with each other, but there was a stone that sat—perfectly fitted—in the connection area, preventing water from the one channel from reaching the other. Just moving that stone would divert the water from the first channel to the second, presumably causing something to fill with water and lever the door aside.

There was no way we could avoid causing some kind of stir here, but maybe we could still avoid combat. Moving carefully around the guards, I positioned myself near the door, while Jodi walked over and considered the fitted stone. I saw her shrug, then stick the claw end of her crowbar in and lever the stone out. To my surprise, she then picked the stone up and carried it over, joining me by the door. Jodi's a big woman, and because of her very active lifestyle she's a lot stronger than her slender build would lead you to think. Still, I wouldn't have thought she could handle that large a stone so readily.

I didn't give it much thought, however, because I was watching to see how the *Lisharithada* would react. As far as I could tell, we weren't so much invisible as just effectively a blind spot in their field of vision. Humans have a blind spot in each eye, but we virtually never notice them. Our brains cover up their existence, filling in the area with appropriately non-distracting "stuff" so we perceive our field of view as being complete and uninterrupted even though there's a significant hole in it. Apparently the same phenomenon applied here. They simply weren't *aware* that anything was happening where we were.

"Why didn't you just move it to the 'open' position?"

"Because I could just see the comedy routine if I did! They can't see me, right? So they see the water going, come over to check it out, I back away so they don't go blind and realize what's up, they push it back in place, door doesn't finish opening, I schlep back over and push the rock: lather, rinse, repeat."

By now the guards had noticed the water flow had shifted and were gathering around the valve area. I couldn't understand the words, but the tones were so very familiar I could almost interpret it anyway.

What the heck's going on? Hey, where's the damn rock? Who's the joker? Dammit, that's going to stick the door open!

And open was exactly what the door was doing, rising up smoothly on its unseen lever arm which was now weighted down by the water pouring into some hidden bucket. I had to concede Jodi had done the right thing. Given how ponderously slow these doors opened, we'd never have gotten it open wide enough to get through without Jodi's tactic, at least not without ending up having to lay the guards out. "Good call, Jodi."

Jodi looked smug. She does "smug" awfully well, too; it's probably her worst major character flaw.

The new tunnel branched out to left and right; we took the right-hand branch, which was narrower than the tunnels we'd been in earlier. Jodi stowed away the crowbar and got the longer, straighter rod of steel that she'd made up for a weapon—like a blunt sword with a wooden and leather-wrapped handle. There weren't quite as many *Lisharithada* in this corridor as there had been in the other, but it was enough smaller that neither of us had much hope we could continue undetected for very long. We were getting close to the ritual area, though. Just maybe we'd get away with it.

Suddenly a mob of fifteen of them came charging down towards us, weapons out.

I was in the lead. They were coming so fast I figured I could hurdle the first line of them and sow confusion in the middle, so I jumped just as they got to me.

I damn near cracked my head open on the cavern roof, which wasn't less than twenty feet up. I was so completely stunned that I landed like a sack of potatoes. I had to be helped up by Jodi, who had followed my example but kept her head a bit more.

I looked back; we had leapt completely over the entire troop, which was continuing on its headlong charge. Whatever they were after, it wasn't us. "Son of a . . . How the hell did we *do* that?!"

"Well, isn't it obvious, genius? That *H'adamant* stuff works! How else do you think I could have hauled that bloody great stone. What? Do I look like a lady weightlifter?"

The look of chagrin combined with outrage on Jodi's face was comical, even under the circumstances. With her elegant, fine-boned features, she looks about as far removed from "lady weightlifter" as possible.

But I didn't dare even crack a smile. "This could take some getting used to," I said gruffly. "We'd better be careful about really pushing ourselves."

"Wonder where those guys were going?"

I thought about it. "Only one real possibility, I'd guess: Rokhaset's kept his word and followed our timing. They're drawing off the *Lisharithada*'s forces. Who else could be down here that they'd be chasing with armed men?"

"Point. Unless they have really tough mice."

The hallway curved around a bit farther to the right. As we rounded the corner, we could see our luck had just run out.

The next room—a pretty darn large one, decorated with flowstone and helictites in one corner—was filled with *Lisharithada*, all armed, ready for the Nomes to try their assault.

There was no way we could cross that room without fighting. Even with the superhuman strength the *H'adamant* elixir seemed to have conferred on us, we couldn't even jump halfway across, and we'd get way too close to a lot of them on the way for them to ignore it.

"This is it, Jodi."

She took a firm grip on the handle of her weapon. "You know, we don't actually have any proof that these are the bad guys."

"What?"

"Rokhaset seems nice and all, but he could still be handing us a line. Or even just turning things around. His people could be the ones making the quakes, and these guys the poor schmucks he's setting up for the fall."

I stared at her with my mouth open for a moment. "Well, god*damn* it, girl, y'all chose a hell of a time t' come up with that theory!"

She shook her head. "I don't really believe it myself, Clint . . . but, *oy vey*, we're here about to declare war on a bunch of people we've never met, all on the say-so of someone we just met day before yesterday."

I guess I wouldn't have been so aggravated if I didn't share her worry, somewhere deep down. We really didn't have any proof of what Rokhaset said, and with the *makatdireskovi's* demonstrated ability to interpret and help Rokhaset express our language like a native-born actor . . .

"So what th' hell do y'all want to do? Sorry, Jodi, but—damnation! Ain't we kind of committed now?"

We dodged a couple runners coming from the other direction. Jodi bit her lip. "I guess we are. I just . . . it hit me, when we were about to walk in and start beating up these poor *schlemiels* who can't even see us."

We'd been so focused on our dilemma that we'd only subconsciously noted the increase in the gabbling language around us. Now it reached a crescendo that broke through our indecision as, suddenly, another detachment of *Lisharithada* burst out of the room in front of us.

There was no chance to dodge or jump. They plowed straight into Jodi and me, knocking us down before they tumbled to the ground themselves in blinded consternation. Scrambling to my feet, I swung my steel at the next *Lisharithada* soldier with all my strength.

The bar bent on impact as though it'd been a willow wand instead of a half-inch of spring steel, picked up the rock-man and flung him a full ten feet backward. A crumpled, oozing line showed where the steel had caught him, as my weapon rebounded into straightness again. Jodi's matching blow knocked over her opponent and the two behind him. Crystal-edged swords chopped blindly at us. I parried one so hard it shattered, raining stone fragments everywhere, but a second one, swung flat and hard, got through my guard.

I staggered sideways, my side on fire. "That hurt!" I snarled, and backhanded the *Lisharithada* who'd hit me hard enough to send him tumbling head over heels. They were trying to crowd in and find us, and I figured giving them that advantage would be bad. "Jodi—into the big cave!"

"Got you!"

We could maneuver better in there, even though there were more opponents. With our height, reach, and effective invisibility—not to mention our magnified strength—our weapons started to take an awful toll. Every swing I made put one of the enemy down—broken legs, shattered chests, crushed skull or arms—and Jodi matched me swing for swing. Worse for them, even when they hit us it didn't smash our bones or cut our limbs off. The blows stung, sometimes really hurt, and I could feel bruises, but nothing at all like the damage they ought to be doing. Two of their guard-*seradatho* scuttled towards me, met the steel coming the other way and flew twisting through the air, shedding pieces as they went.

There was something utterly macabre and horrid about it all. These rock-men were desperately fighting something they couldn't see, something even stronger and tougher than they were—that killed and maimed them, broke their weapons, moved like lightning, and smashed aside any defense. I felt a little sick as we continued to fight our way towards the far side of the room, where just one door stood between us and the ritual room Rokhaset had told us we would find. Even if we were fighting enemies of our people, this was their home, and we were the invaders, slaughtering them without warning, without even showing them the faces of their adversaries. It was as if Jodi and I were the monsters in some kind of underground legend—the rock-people's equivalent of trolls or werewolves.

Still, sheer numbers count for an awful lot. For every one I took down, I could see another one running forward—sometimes two. And while one blow from their weapons wasn't enough to take us down—or even five—in the end you can beat a man to death with a rolled-up newspaper if you hit him often enough.

Two more *Lisharithada* went down, then three of them jumped me and I staggered. A fourth, knocked reeling by Jodi, fell down and tripped me. The three on top were blind, but now they could feel someone under them. They were punching and kicking for all they were worth, their shrieks carrying terror and revulsion along with anger.

"*Clint!*" I heard Jodi scream, and a barrage of impacts erupted from her direction. Two of the ones on me suddenly departed involuntarily, and the third let go and backed off. I got painfully to my feet and smacked a *seradatho* into its handlers.

Jodi's eyes held a desperation I'd never seen before. "We're not going to make it, *tei-yerinkeh*." She almost never used that word; it meant "sweetheart" or "dearest one," but it was a private thing, a silly little private word we used only alone together.

I looked over my shoulder. We weren't even halfway across the room, and in the dimming light—half the LEDs on our lights were broken now—it looked like even more *Lisharithada* were coming in to reinforce the others. She was probably right . . . The ring of *Lisharithada* that had drawn away for a moment was gathering itself for another lunge.

I shook my head. "Maybe, but damn-all if I'm givin' up." I hit the transducer switch. "YEEE-HA! C'mon, then, let's see if y'all can take a Slade!"

And in the stunned moment as the *Lisharithada* heard our voices for the first time, another voice boomed out from across the great cavern:

"Well said and well met again, Clinton Slade!"

14. THE SOUND OF MUSIC

No sound had ever been so welcome as that deep, reassuring voice. "Rokhaset! You made it!" Jodi shouted triumphantly, taking three *Lisharithada* out with the accompanying swing.

"Indeed, Jodi Goldman." I could now make out that at least part of what I'd taken for reinforcements of the *Lisharithada* were Rokhaset's assault forces, driving towards us like a wedge against the increasingly desperate *Lisharithada*. "And it gives me great joy to see that not only have you arrived, but that also the *mikhsteri H'adamant* has worked surpassingly well on you."

"OW!" I shoved the one that had just hit me out of the way. "Yeah, and without it we'd have been dead before we got here. Great stuff."

The enemy were now in serious disarray. They couldn't decide whether the two invisible slayers or the larger number of *Nowëthada* were the biggest threat, and that made them hesitate at the wrong time. Jodi and I turned and started plowing our way towards the door on the far side, knowing that Rokhaset and his troops were backing us up and if the ones behind us tried to drag us down, he'd carve right through them and get 'em off our backs.

Now there wasn't any mistaking the panic in the voices of the *Lisharithada*. The situation had gone from bad to impossible. There just weren't enough of them left to deal with Rokhaset's forces on top of the unknown, invisible killers that had devastated their guarding force. Seeing how Rokhaset and his people proceeded onward—steadily, but nowhere near as fast or efficient as our devastating attack—it was pretty clear that he'd told the truth about just how little chance he and his people had stood alone. That, to me, confirmed we'd chosen right to take his word on this mission. There wasn't any way he'd expected events to take the turn they had, but he'd clearly planned on this assault anyway. Plus, his people had had several chances to do us in at different points, and hadn't.

Suddenly, the *Lisharithada* morale broke. The ones in front of us threw down their weapons and sprang aside, running for the exits—there were, I could see, three ways out of here besides the sealed door we were headed for. And even the ones behind us and around Rokhaset's people were now fleeing, stampeding out the doors with desperate speed.

"Well, I think they've decided that's enough."

Rokhaset joined us. His posture had not relaxed. "They do not usually retreat even when being beaten."

"And how often have you had invisible, superhuman, apparently invincible assistance? C'mon, Rokhaset, everyone has a breaking point."

"True enough, Clinton Slade. I find your presence unnerving, and you are my ally. Perhaps indeed it is that invisible assistance which overwhelms their courage."

"Last door. I hope we can get it open from this side."

Rokhaset nodded deliberately. "I assure you it can be opened, especially by those assembled here. Be prepared; the interior guard will have been alerted, and they will fight to the end."

"Let 'er rip. Let's blow this joint and see if we can get home in one piece."

The Nomes gathered around the door, poking at the mechanism, which was apparently jammed. After a jabbering conference, Rokhaset turned back to us. "The door is not entirely disabled. They did not have the time to do so, and those inside cannot do so without considerable effort. Stand by; we shall open the door—now!"

Something broke inside the wall—we could hear it and feel the vibration through the soles of our boots—and the door ground its way upwards. The doorway to our destination was open.

Stepping forward, Jodi and I peered in. It was a low but tremendously wide room, maybe ten feet high but with regular buttress columns supporting a span so large that our weakened lights couldn't reach the other side, even with the increased sensitivity of our eyes. At regular intervals around the room were crystalline shapes of bizarre design. The nearest one was a sort of curved double-trumpet shape rising from one side of a six-foot-high dais, thirty feet across, carved in a spiral fashion with rippled indentations along it. I started for it, raising my bar and watching for the interior guard.

No one came forward, no attackers, nothing. "Rokhaset? Where's the welcome wagon?"

"I admit my bewilderment, Clinton Slade. I cannot—"

But at that moment, the dais began to uncurl. The crystalline shape sat at the crest of a head fully five feet long, armed with black-shining spines, cutting blades of blue stone, a crushing maw, and grasping talons. It gave voice to a grinding screech like the unoiled hinges of Hell and turned towards us.

"*Magon!*" Rokhaset gasped. His shocked cry was echoed by his fellows, all of whom, the Nome King included, began backing away as fast as they could.

"Figures." I stared at the monstrous thing as it continued to uncoil. "They brought one here as a last-ditch defense."

The *Magon* shrieked again, and a steady humming began to emanate from it as it stalked towards us on many sets of legs.

"*Matturan!*" I heard Rokhaset shout. "Run, all of you, for we cannot fight if we cannot see!"

"Well, I can see perfectly—what the . . . *YOW!*"

My steel weapon had brushed my hand; that fleeting contact had burned me.

"*Gevalt!*" Jodi cursed.

The zipper on my wetsuit was heating up. If you have never experienced the sensation of a rapidly-heating zipper, my advice is simple: avoid it at all costs.

Jodi grabbed me and dragged me backward, away, running as fast as we could from the *Magon*. We both tore the earphones from our heads, as they were starting to burn our ears.

"The damn thing's radiating electromagnetic waves!" Jodi said disbelievingly. "That's why it makes the Nomes blind—it's overloading their senses on some level. But for us, it's inducing eddy currents and heating every bit of metal on us!"

"Damn! Damn, damn, *damn!* No wonder the *Lisharithada* bugged out. They knew this thing was waiting back there as a last-ditch weapon." We stopped for a breather on the far side of the cavern we'd been fighting in for so long. Two of the exits had been closed off, but one was still open. That gave me an idea.

"Hey, Rokhaset! Our real goal's to get inside that room and break up all the crystal things, right?"

"Correct."

Eric Flint and Ryk E. Spoor

"Well, that being the case, why don't we have one group of us keep the thing chasin' us, and the other group runs inside? That *Magon* thing sure doesn't look up to opening doors, so if we can all get inside ahead of it and close the door, we're set."

"A worthy plan," Rokhaset said after a pause.

"Why isn't Rokhaset answering?" Jodi demanded. "Is he okay?"

"He *is* answering. I guess my electronics survived, but yours fried."

"Some of them, anyway. Lights and all are still working."

I glanced in the direction we'd come from. Nothing was moving in the range of the lights. "Speaking of that, I'm swapping out for the spare lights and new batteries. I can't see the thing at all."

That did the trick nicely, but I didn't like what I saw. "Shoot. The darn thing's stopped with its head right in the doorway. Rokhaset, y'all said these things were hard to control, but looks to me like this one understands 'guard dog' just fine."

Jodi gazed at it speculatively. "Wonder what its range is?"

"We should probably find out. Though to be honest I dunno what we're going to do. My pistol's just a popgun to something like that, and no way I'm gonna get close enough to hit it with the explosives—hell, I was lucky the detonators and my pistol rounds didn't go off when it started doing its metal-heating trick."

"Well, I don't have any explosives on me, and most of my stuff that's going to fry is already toasted." Jodi dashed forward before I could stop her.

The *Magon* raised its head a bit as she got closer, and that eerie, high-pitched, monotonous hum began again. Jodi snatched up her weapon, which was about thirty feet from the thing, and ran back, juggling it like a hot potato until she got back to me and dropped it on the floor to cool.

"*Oy!* Looks like it's got a range around seventy-five feet. At least, it didn't seem to be cooling off until I got out about that far. You didn't feel anything back here, did you?"

I shook my head. "Nothing. Though I'd bet the range for just blinding our Nome friends is much longer."

"You are correct, Clinton Slade. We dare not get even as close as you are now to the *Magon*. Although . . . Perhaps, if we were to all rush it at once, we might still defeat it. There are twelve of us all told, plus the two of you."

"No, you're outta your mind, Rokhaset! That thing's even bigger'n you said; I think I eyeballed it at something close on eighty feet long. It'd kick our asses even if y'all weren't blind, which you will be." I studied the thing from our current distance, about a hundred and fifty feet away. "Jodi, do you want to try that run again and see if you can get my weapon too?"

She looked at me. "You've got something else in mind, haven't you?"

"Maybe. More a matter of I need to get a better look at something." I moved forward until I was about a hundred feet away from the thing.

"Here goes nothing." Jodi sprinted back in. The grotesque head rose, the humming started up again, and Jodi gave vent to Yiddish curses as her clothing started to heat up. She had to get within twenty feet of the *Magon* to get my weapon, and at her closest approach the thing stirred uneasily, almost began to move forward, jaws and grinder working.

But I'd noticed something else. I focused my flashlight squarely on the crystalline growth on the *Magon*'s forehead as Jodi sprinted back. Sure enough, the light looked vaguely defocused until she got far enough out and the humming sound faded, and then the reflection was as sharp as could be.

"I think I've found its transmission antenna."

"The things I do for love! What? Where?"

"That crystal thing on its head. That humming noise coincides with its vibration." I shook my head. "I suppose I could try to shoot the thing off, but it's a sucky target in this light and at this distance."

Jodi stared at it with a look of revelation that startled me.

"Jodi? Sweetheart, what is it?"

"Clint, tell me: doesn't that thing look almost exactly like a couple of wineglasses from here?"

I looked. "Well, yeah, it does. So?"

"I'd put that hum right up around my high B."

My mouth dropped open and stayed that way. "You can't be serious!"

"I'll bet you twenty bucks it'll work."

"You're nuts! You'd need to get right up to it—twenty, thirty feet at the outside—and it's looking kinda antsy already."

"So, like you have a better idea, Mr. Genius?"

I thought about it. "No," I finally muttered. "But hold on a second. I'd better get stuff ready, in case this crazy idea of yours does work."

I pulled stuff from the pack, sorted it out, fitted things together, checked the connections. "Okay." I looked over at the monstrous creature and turned, grabbing Jodi tight. "You be damn careful, y'hear? I ain't lookin' to see you eaten by some rockworm."

The slight quiver in her voice answered my concern. "Hey, don't worry, it's no big deal. You should see the rats on a New York subway."

"I *have* seen the rats on a New York subway. They aren't anywhere near as bad as—"

She clucked her tongue disparagingly. "That was just Manhattan, you tourist. I'm talking about Queens. Now stop distracting me."

She took a deep breath and hummed to herself for a few moments, running scales up and down, loosening her throat and lungs so they could deliver when needed. As she did so, she started stripping off all the extraneous metal. Her backpack hit the floor as she started a run of *do-re-mi* and her shirt and pants (with metal rivets) joined it a few moments later as she ran back down the scale, followed by the wetsuit.

Being human—okay, male human—I could at least appreciate the view, which was magnificent even if stopping *just* short of being indecent. Jodi's sports bra and panties had no metal in them, so she left them on. Still, there was a definite exotic charm in the setting, especially with the waiting monster in the background. Any fantasy illustrator in the world would have been in seventh heaven.

Jodi stood still for a moment, muscles just a bit too tense, then took a deep breath and started walking forward.

As before, once she got within seventy feet, the creature raised its head and started humming. But this time Jodi wasn't wearing anything metal to be affected. She kept moving forward slowly, forty feet, thirty, twenty-five, twenty . . .

At twenty feet, the *Magon* hissed and moved slightly. Jodi stopped and opened her mouth. A pure note issued forth, one matching the eerie hum precisely in pitch. The hum instantly sounded louder than ever, and Jodi's voice responded, increasing volume steadily.

The *Magon* must have encountered caverns in which it had heard feedback. The hum started to fade for a moment as it stopped generation. But nothing had ever tried this trick on it before; as Jodi made a step forward, its instincts forced it to begin the defensive signal generation again.

Jodi's face was as set as a marble statue, giving out an unending, unwavering tone that I knew could not be sustained much longer, a crescendo of echoing sound that was answered in the swiftly-building hum that she was trying to drive out of control. The *Magon* moved jerkily, trying to shake its head and drive away an indescribable sensation, starting a lunge forward but drawing back as the movement increased the resonance. Even from this distance I saw Jodi's face changing color slightly, reddening from the effort of wringing the last dregs of air from her lungs to maintain the feedback cycle. She was running out of air, it wasn't going to work—

And then the sound of her own pure voice echoed out from behind me, doubled and redoubled, as the *Nowëthada*, having caught on to her plan, all joined together to imitate the same precise sound. Though they were much farther away, there were twelve of them, and they were putting all the strength into it they could; with their ability to imitate other sounds perfectly, they did exactly what was needed. They maintained the resonance as the *Magon* gave a frustrated whine and finally moved, in fits and starts, towards Jodi.

But by maintaining the resonance, the Nomes had given Jodi a breather. She backed up two steps, her lungs refilled, and this time her voice seemed to split the room with a single note of high-pitched thunder. The resonant hum from the *Magon* rose with her volume, becoming louder, the creature scrabbling now to reach its own forehead with claws just a bit too short— and the crystal antenna exploded with enough force to send shards flying thirty feet.

The *Magon* gave a shriek that pierced my ears like an icepick and lunged at Jodi; no longer under control, just berserk and out to kill the one that hurt it. Jodi ran.

I stood still and let her run past me. As the *Magon* followed—ignoring me completely in its mania to get Jodi—I swung the iron at one of its legs hard enough to break it. There was no heating; Jodi's trick had ended that problem. The monstrous centipedal creature skidded to a halt and whipped around, screaming at me—and that's when I pitched the ball in my other hand down its throat.

For a moment only I saw it, sparkling silvery in the LED light with its duct-taped surface. Then I flung myself flat behind a low, domelike stalactite.

The blast deafened me and shattered helictites sixty feet away. When I rose up, I could see that the *Magon* was writhing on the floor, headless and dying. All Jodi and I had to do was dance like madmen to stay out of the way of the rocky coils until they juddered slowly into stillness. Two pounds of C-4 makes for a hell of a case of indigestion.

Rokhaset and the other Nomes moved forward slowly. Even though they didn't have expressions, everything about the way they moved shouted out their incredulity. "Clinton Slade, Jodi Goldman . . . you have defeated a *Magon*. I did not think it possible."

"*Nishtkefelecht*, it's nothing. Without you singing backup, my main performance would've bombed. We did it together."

"Perhaps, perhaps. Still, such a thing has not been done in my memory."

"Enough time to congratulate later. Let's finish this job and get out of here before they come back to check on us."

As we turned towards the door, a quiver ran through the floor. Then another, stronger shake that jangled the remaining helictites.

"*Jh'amos!* They know we have won out here. They seek to complete the ritual now, though it will be slightly weakened!"

"Oh, no they don't!"

Into the room we ran. There were some guards now, running to stop us in these last desperate minutes, but this time I had the pistol out and was shooting. It probably wouldn't kill them, but the impact of the slugs startled them, knocked them off balance, broke armor where it hit. I ran past, kicking over a tall stone with an intricate crystal atop it, and then I saw him—like Rokhaset, bigger than his subjects, surrounded by crystalline structures, mumbling incomprehensible sounds. His personal guard swung at me, but I bowled him over and grabbed the *Lisharithada* ruler, swinging him right up against the wall. "Rokhaset!" I shouted. "Tell 'em to cut it out right now, or I'm about to break their king in half!"

Rokhaset and the *Lisharithada* exchanged hurried words. "They say it is all over for them in any case, now that you monsters have found them. They might as well take us all with them."

"It's all over! Tell 'em, Rokhaset—we only got here because you showed us, and we ain't told anyone else!"

A shattering sound told me Jodi was finishing off the crystals. The *Lisharithada* king struggled desperately in my grip; then, as the sound of crashing crystal faded, went limp.

"It would seem, Clinton Slade, that he has recognized a losing position, now that Jodi Goldman has destroyed the channeling crystals."

I dropped the king. "Okay. So they can't do the earthquake now?"

"No, Clint. It will be a long time before they can regrow such a mass of channeling crystals and even attempt such a ritual again."

"Good. Let's go get your stuff, Jodi, and go home."

The *Lisharithada* king suddenly whirled around, yanking a long staff of stone capped with a green-glowing gem from its hiding place in the depression from which I'd yanked him. I threw up my hands instinctively, but the gem hit me like a wrecking ball combined with a cattle prod. Concussion and seething energy catapulted me backwards, twitching.

The room erupted in renewed combat as the king directed his next attack, a sickly emerald bolt of energy, straight at Jodi. She tried to block it with her steel rod and had no more success than I had. Seeing her collapse, I tried desperately to get up, but my legs and arms wouldn't move.

Rokhaset roared something I couldn't make out, and there was a confused exchange of lightnings, red and green clashing as though the rainbow was having an internal debate. A glittering, three-crested head loomed above me, then fell as Rokhaset's own scepter came down on it.

Everything was dim, silent. I wondered why it was growing so dark, realized that I must be losing consciousness.

"Clinton Slade! Can you hear me?"

I made a supreme effort, managed to force out the word, "Yes."

"It is over. Their ruler is dead, they will have to select a new one, and we can escape."

"Guess . . . over for us . . . too."

"No, Clinton Slade. We shall bring you home."

I felt strong, slender rods of stone . . . Nome arms . . . slide under me. "Jodi . . ."

"We have her too. Save your strength."

I tried to tell him that I wasn't lying down here while Jodi might be hurt, but my lips wouldn't move. The light faded, and then everything was dark and I fell away into nothingness.

15. SOME SLIGHT SIDE-EFFECTS.

Consciousness returned in fits and starts. I vaguely remembered shouting Nomish voices, and a feeling of sudden comfort overwhelming me as we entered *Nowëmosdet* again. Darkness giving way to light and Mamma crying. Being forced to drink something that stank like rotten eggs and tasted . . . well, it was a good thing I couldn't fight it then or someone woulda gotten hurt.

I opened my eyes. It was dim in the room. Shades were pulled over the windows. I tried to get up, but just getting to a sitting position took the wind out of me. "Hello?" I called.

The door flew open and Mamma ran in. "Clint? Oh, thank the Lord, Clint, you're awake! How do you feel, boy?"

"Like I've been pulled through a knothole and wrung out. And like I could eat a bear whole, without salt."

Tears glinted in her eyes. "Well, I'm sure we can find something to eat for you! Just stay there and take it easy and I'll be right back!"

"Jodi, Mamma! What about Jodi?"

Mamma hesitated. "She hasn't woken up yet, Clint, but now that you've come back to us I'm sure she'll be up and about in no time."

"But she's alive?" I felt a huge weight lift off my chest.

"She is indeed alive, Clinton Slade." Rokhaset entered the room. "Did I not give my word that we would get you home and that we had Jodi as well?"

"Yeah, and I didn't doubt you meant it . . . but sometimes the world can make liars of the best of us." Mamma, seeing that I had someone to talk to, headed on out, presumably to round up some food.

It suddenly dawned on me that I was not wearing any transducers. I glanced around and saw speakers on the bedside table. Obviously someone had decided to distribute the ability to talk to the Nome King around the house. Probably Adam, I guessed.

"She is recovering, I assure you. Though it was indeed a near thing for you both. It took the medicine of both worlds to bring you back from the edge of death."

"So you were the one making me drink that stuff."

"You needed the *Nowë H'wadalo*, the True Fire of Her spirit, and the elixir gave it to you. *Mishtarkistekh' orametanerala* intended for both Jodi Goldman and yourself to never return from the paths below the Earth, and tried to extinguish the fire of life within you. Had you been of our people, you would have died on the spot; had you been ordinary *Tennathada*, I doubt it would have affected you any more than an ordinary blow. But by being brought closer to *Nowë* by the *H'adamant* elixir, you were in a unique state and his attempt to destroy you neither entirely failed nor entirely succeeded."

"Dang. Slades don't usually do anything halfway. Well, better half dead than all dead, that's what I say."

"That would be my assessment as well."

"So . . . no big quakes then?"

Rokhaset nodded slowly. "For now, no. Yet it is true that the *Lisharithada* shall recover in time, and the Earth still builds its tensions which will need careful release if they are not to harness its strength for destruction. But that will be a problem for a later day. Your deeds this time have struck fear and confusion into them, and there is no need to worry; I shall know when they begin to think of the great rituals again."

Mamma came in with a tray piled with everything from soup to drumsticks. "Now that's enough jawing, Rokhaset. Let my boy eat."

I ate, as directed; by the time I was done, my eyelids were sagging again. I don't really remember putting the tray down.

* * *

When I woke again, it was nighttime, the moon shining through the slits in the window and lighting the room up so it looked almost like daylight. I tried to move and found I could get up, though I felt like Grandpa on a bad day. I tottered across the room and almost fell over Evangeline, who steadied me. "Careful, Clint. Nice to see you up, though. You wanna see Jodi, I bet."

"You'd win that bet."

"Well, c'mon. Mamma would probably try to keep you in bed, but that wouldn't be fair."

Evangeline led me down the hall—which seemed 'round about five times longer than usual—and opened the door to Jodi's room.

Jodi's eyes were open, and I felt tears suddenly well up in my own. I staggered to her bed and hugged her tight. "Jesus, Jodi, I thought we were dead."

"You weren't the only one, boychik. That nasty green light laid me right out."

We sat there for a few moments, just holding each other and absorbing the fact that we were still alive.

"Hey. It just hit me. We saved the world."

"Oy, don't go exaggerating. Just part of the country. Not even the most important part. Manhattan wouldn't have been touched."

I laughed. "Okay, yeah, but . . . in a way, it might not be exaggerating. A big enough disaster to the USA . . . I'm sure the rest of the world economy wouldn't like it either."

"They'd get by. Hey, are you saying it's not enough?"

"Heck no. It's just a lot more impressive to say 'I saved the world' than 'I saved Kentucky, Tennessee, Missouri, southern Illinois, and chunks here and there of a few other states in the area.' "

Jodi thought about it. "Especially where I come from. Most New Yorkers think Kentucky and Tennessee—forget Missouri—are just suburbs of Hoboken."

*　*　*

Over the next few days, Jodi and I got better. Finally we felt like ourselves again and Mamma threw a heck of a party, which Rokhaset attended, wearing his sunglasses and bringing two of his court along—*Tordamilatakituranavasaiko* and *Mesh'atarasamthimajistolath*, whose names were promptly shortened in our *Tennathada* way to Tordamil and Meshatar.

The new arrivals were the first of their people given a connection to the expanded *makatdireskovi* so as to be able to talk with us. It was nice to hear new voices; Meshatar sounded like Lauren Bacall, which certainly helped us remember she was female, as there weren't any clear visible indications of sex among the Nomes. Tordamil had evidently selected Richard Dean Anderson as his voice model, making it occasionally sound as though MacGyver had come to dinner.

The Nomes brought their own food with them, to the family's great interest. Though Mamma realized that making *Nowëthada* dinners would probably be impossible for any of us, she still ended up talking to Tordamil after dinner, trying to understand just what it was that the Nomes did when they "cooked." As Tordamil turned out to be Rokhaset's head *sirakster H'ista*, which apparently meant something between "master chef" and "head shaman or alchemist," he was definitely the one to ask about these things. He was just as interested in our methods of cooking—or at least convincingly faked an interest in it—so the two were kept happily occupied for a long time.

We went out to look around the grounds with Rokhaset after dinner.

"Man, it's nice to be outside again."

"I like caves, but after that long trek, okay, yeah, I'm glad to be aboveground again too."

"I will admit, Clinton Slade, that there are enjoyable aspects to *Tennatu*. You will forgive me, I trust, if I still prefer *Nowëtu*."

"Wouldn't expect anything else, Rokhaset. A man should always love his home best, no matter what sights there are to see elsewhere." I glanced at him. "Speakin' of sights, I thought you people were damn near blind here in the Hollow?"

"We are indeed *matturan* to some extent whenever we are here, Clinton Slade. But other senses can be used to appreciate the world; and it is, I think, not entirely a bad thing for myself and my people to accustom themselves to this, in case they must deal with your people."

"Can't hurt to be ready to deal with it, I guess. But we ain't planning to spread the word about your people around."

Rokhaset nodded emphatically. "As individuals your people have proven to be, as you would say, decent folk. I am however very much afraid that were your country as a whole to become aware of us—and especially of the *Lisharithada*—that it would become a matter for politicians of your sort . . . and eventually for warriors, once they realized what the *Lisharithada* were capable of."

"Oy, no doubt about that one, Rokhaset. They'd be dragging half of you to the labs and declaring war on the other half. Clint may be a backwoods boy, but he's pretty enlightened. There's plenty of other people that'd be perfectly willing to ignore the fact you can talk and just call you monsters."

I didn't want to get off discussing the flaws of the entire human race which Rokhaset, having derived his understanding of us from forty years of TV, was undoubtedly all too aware of. "Besides," I said, "it'd be just plumb stupid of us. The Slades have got some tradin' to do with your people, right?"

We had gotten past the edge of the Hollow now, and Rokhaset was moving a bit more easily. "That is a matter I have been discussing with your family during your convalescence, Clinton Slade. While the initial problem was certainly caused by your blind thievery, even the most reactionary of my people— and make no mistake about it, Jodi Goldman, the *Nowëthada* are just as capable of anger, deliberate prejudice, and judgmental behavior as your own—as I say, even the most reactionary of my people must admit that the two of you risked everything— your lives, your freedom, and your souls—to atone for the involuntary wrongdoings of Winston Slade and his descendants.

"We are, accordingly, quite interested in establishing a peaceful trade between the Slade clan and our own. Yet we still find ourselves at the same impasse that we encountered when first we spoke of this problem."

"What d'you . . . oh, yeah."

"You grasp the issue, Clinton Slade. We have no need for the devices your people manufacture, at least not in any significant quantity, and many of your machines would have to be specifically redesigned to make them worth our while. So the only reasonable trading goods we have are crystals—we supply you with diamonds, as we can, and you bring us gemstones and other crystals which cannot be found in this part of the world. Yet your people are as blind in this area as we are in what you call the visible spectrum. You cannot tell whether a crystal is *hevrat* with life, or is as dead"—he gestured at the brilliantly-sparkling diamond on Jodi's finger—"as that. And clearly you cannot afford to purchase many rough stones, hoping they will be worthwhile, and have them rejected—at least not often."

"Well . . . depends. If your people can shape stones like I've seen, you ought to be able to cut gems to order. That'd raise the value of the reject gems an' we could still recoup."

"Sure he could, Clint," Jodi said, with the air of a teacher explaining something to a really slow student, "but to make it worth his people's while we'd have to, well, make it worth their while . . ."

"D'oh!" I smacked my forehead. "Okay, yeah, that was dumb."

"Alas, Clinton Slade, mine are a busy people indeed and truly we cannot perform much labor for you unless we can establish equitable exchange. I do, however, have one thing to give you."

"Oh?"

He withdrew from the woven-crystal pouch at his side what looked like two medallions suspended from strings made of the same material as his pouch. "As, I suspect, nearly all people, the *Nowëthada* recognize and honor bravery, willingness to aid others, strength in battle, and so on. It took considerable courage for the two of you to come to us, into our stronghold, and hope to make peace—perhaps, if I read your personalities aright, more than it took to face the *Lisharithada* and the *Magon*."

"Well, I don't rightly know about that. Even walking into your throne room wasn't as scary as fighting a stone monster the size of a house. But still, we appreciate the kind words."

"To recognize you for bringing our people together, and standing with us against a common foe, I have had fashioned these amulets. They have little mystical significance to one such as yourself, but similar devices mean a great deal to my people, and I know that you award similar, um, medals, to courageous members of your own species. So take these, at least, as . . . what is the phrase? Ah, yes, as a token of our esteem and gratitude for bringing our sundered peoples together. May we one day find a way to bring peace to the *Lisharithada* as well."

"I'm all for that, though I admit to not bein' overly hopeful." We each stooped low to let Rokhaset, who once more had clearly watched the similar rituals on movies and TV shows, put the medallions around our necks. Straightening up, we then got a chance to look at them.

"*Oooy!*" Jodi breathed. "Rokhaset, these are just beautiful!"

I had to agree. The medallions were shaped—or maybe grown—transparent crystals with traces of glittering metal in them that looked like gold, surrounding a core of what had to be solid silver, covered with intricate designs that looked like completed versions of the symbols we'd seen on the Throne Room walls. I wondered if silver gave them problems to work, or if it was just the ferromagnetics that did. Overshadowing all the other features, though, was the crystal set in the very center. It, too, was transparent, but it didn't merely pass light; it radiated light, a soft but unmistakable polychromatic glow that pulsed and flickered gently like a candle in the gentlest of breezes. As I admired it in the slowly-gathering dusk, I realized the whole medallion had a faint glow to it, though nothing like the glorious luminance from that central stone.

"What *is* that stone, Rokhaset? It's incredible!"

"I am surprised, Jodi Goldman, Clinton Slade. How can you not recognize the stones over which we nearly shed blood? They are *H'adamant*, of course. The only appropriate choice."

"Okay," I said, "but what'd you do to 'em to make 'em glow like that?"

Rokhaset froze, looking almost comical. "Glow? Clinton Slade, I assure you—we have done nothing to them at all, save to shape them so they are faceted in a way that would reflect the light pleasingly for your eyes."

"But . . . these look nothing at all like Jodi's diamond! Well, yeah, they're both transparent, but . . ."

I trailed off, a chill going down my spine as I realized what I was saying.

"Clinton Slade," Rokhaset said, with a quiet intensity that showed how serious he was, "Look carefully at me and tell me what you see."

We stared at Rokhaset. "Oh, my," Jodi whispered.

In the dimming light, looking hard at Rokhaset, we could see that he glowed like our medallions. It was dim, yet with a sense of being contained—like being in a dark room and seeing the glow under the door from the brightly-lit hall beyond.

It was only then that I glanced at my watch, remembering just when we'd started eating. Twilight? At this time of night it ought to be damn near pitch black. Yet it only seemed to be late twilight—easy enough to see in, even if the shadows were pretty thick under the trees.

"*Nowë Ro'vahari,*" Rokhaset said in a tone of reverence. "Such things are mentioned in legends, from before the *Makurada Demagon*, but how they happened none could say. Perhaps the *mikhsteri H'adamant*, combined with the change in our peoples, has done this itself; perhaps the treacherous attack of the *Lisharithada* ruler, or our desperate treatments of its effects on you, has wrought this transformation. But somehow

Nowë has seen fit to make you *turan*, at least in some way, as we do."

"Then I gotta apologize, Rokhaset. I thought you were overreacting when you realized we couldn't see what happened when *H'adamant* died. Now . . . I think maybe y'all almost didn't get mad enough."

I wondered what else had changed about us. "I sure hope there aren't any nasty side-effects waiting. Don't want to go blind around metal, that's for sure."

"It is as *Nowë* wills it, Clinton Slade. Yet it would seem to me that her blessing is, for you, working as your normal sight, only . . . more so. It should, therefore, not be so sensitive to *H'kuraden* as ours, if at all."

"I'm going to have to get to the lab!" Jodi exclaimed. "Clint, an entirely new sensing modality—even if we're the only ones with it, just imagine what we could learn this way!"

"Whoa, whoa. One thing at a time. The important thing is that this solves our trading problem."

Rokhaset laughed. "We spoke and the World heard us, and answered. So it has ever been, Clinton Slade, in the times when it was crucial. *Nowë* is pleased with you, Jodi Goldman, Clinton Slade. It is important to Her that we be friends. So She has provided."

I was starting to realize that our pragmatic friend was also about as religious as a preacher. But if he wanted to see this as a miracle, what'd it matter? Heck, he might even be right! "Let's just hope it doesn't wear off."

Rokhaset nodded slowly. "Yet this, in itself, gives us an answer. If the effects of the elixir remain with you for this long—even if only the senses are affected—then at the worst you merely need take one before you go on a . . . shopping trip. With careful planning, even taking into consideration the costs we would have to charge you for the *mikhsteri H'adamant*, I am sure it would remain a very profitable venture on both sides."

He tilted his head in that birdlike fashion. "Clinton Slade, I must return home now. In the wake of our battle I have spent far too much time here, though I do not regret that time. I have informed Meshatar and Tordamil that we must go; they are taking their leave of your family. Send them my apologies, but I can no longer ignore my people. Please, come visit us soon, however. I would be honored to entertain your family in my home."

We shook hands and went with him to Winston's Cave—where the iron grid had been removed and the handholds down replaced by *Nowëthada* stone-shaping. Meshatar and Tordamil came hurrying up just as Rokhaset entered, so we got to say goodbye to them too. Then we headed back down the path.

"So, Clint . . ."

"What?"

"We'll have to be pretty careful."

"You mean to not let people know we can see in the dark—and maybe see other things, too? Yeah."

"More than that."

I turned to see what she was talking about, as we emerged from Winston's Gap. "Holy Mother of God!"

Jodi was carrying the gate, which had been left way off to the side as no one had wanted to carry it down the hill at the time. It weighed in at something like five hundred pounds.

"You just better hope that it doesn't wear off while you're pulling stunts like that, girl!"

"I'd bet I'd feel it happening."

I reached out, wondering if I had the same ludicrous strength. She relinquished her hold, and I hefted the mass of steel. The gate felt more like forty, fifty pounds, if that. "Well, shit fire and save matches. You know, this is even weirder'n it looks. I haven't felt like Superman at home, an' the chairs I was draggin' into place before dinner didn't feel any lighter, so what gives?"

Jodi the scientist answered. "We'll just have to experiment and find out. Maybe Rokhaset's a little off—maybe these abilities *will* go away when we're around a lot of iron."

I lifted the gate a bit higher. "Counterpoint: just what is it I'm holding, then?"

Jodi studied it, frowning. "Okay," she admitted a bit grudgingly, "I'd say that counts as a falsified theory. Maybe it's expectations; we don't get the high-end strength and toughness unless we're either trying to use it, or maybe panicked into using it. We can test that. And see whether it's decreasing or staying steady. Remember, we never had any chance to test out exactly how strong we were back in the *Lisharithada* caverns. So it may be—probably is—slowly fading in effect. We just need to know how long it'll take."

I chuckled suddenly. "Nope. I can tell you it's going to be staying steady. However it happened, we've got 'em for the rest of our lives."

"What? Clint, how can you say that?" She stared at me as my smile widened.

"Because it comes from the *H'adamant* elixir."

"And? What's your point?"

I couldn't help letting my smile turn into an evil grin. "Why, Jodi, everyone knows that."

I paused for dramatic effect.

"Diamonds are forever."

Made in the USA
Columbia, SC
11 July 2020